WE TOTALLY SAW THIS COMING. . . .

"Bad news, guys!" Their father walked down the aisle toward them. "We can't land in Svalbard because there's too much ice on the runway . . . so we're going to have to jump out of the plane!"

Celia turned to her brother. "You totally jinxed us," she said.

"What? How did I do that?" Oliver replied.

"You brought up jumping out of a plane!" said Celia. "On TV, you can't talk about jumping out of a plane while you're on a plane. Because then you'll have to jump out of it!"

"No," said Oliver. "You can't talk about *not wanting* to jump out of a plane. That's the rule! And you said, 'I don't want Oliver jumping out of the plane. I don't want anyone jumping out of the plane.' So this is your fault."

"That's not the rule," said Celia.

"Yes it is," said Oliver. "I know the rules."

"But this isn't TV," said his father.

"The rules are the same," he said.

"If you say so," Dr. Navel said. "When I was your age, we had these crazy things called books."

"When you were our age, did your parents make you jump out of an airplane?" Oliver asked.

"Well no," said Dr. Navel. "I guess times change."

"I guess so." Celia scowled.

OTHER BOOKS YOU MAY ENJOY

WE
SLED WITH DRAGONS

WE SLED WITH DRAGONS

AN ACCIDENTAL ADVENTURE

C. Alexander London

With art by **Jonny Duddle**

PUFFIN BOOKS
An Imprint of Penguin Group (USA) Inc.

PUFFIN BOOKS
An imprint of Penguin Young Readers Group
Published by the Penguin Group
Penguin Group (USA) Inc.
375 Hudson Street
New York, New York 10014, U.S.A.

USA / Canada / UK / Ireland / Australia / New Zealand / India / South Africa / China
Penguin Books Ltd, Registered Offices: 80 Strand, London WC2R 0RL, England

For more information about the Penguin Group visit www.penguin.com

Published by Puffin Books, an imprint of Penguin Young Readers Group, 2013

LIBRARY OF CONGRESS CATALOGING-IN-PUBLICATION DATA IS AVAILABLE UPON REQUEST
Puffin Books ISBN 978-0-14-242694-4

Printed in the United States of America

1 3 5 7 9 10 8 6 4 2

For my own Indiana Jones
and our adventures yet to come

CONTENTS

WE
SLED WITH
DRAGONS

1
WE PLAN THE PLAN

"WHOSE BOOTY?" OLIVER Navel asked for the third time, as their small boat bobbed gently on the waves and lights twinkled on the shore.

"It's no one's booty!" His twin sister, Celia, groaned at him. "It's Djibouti! It's the name of the city. *Jib-boot-tee!* Djibouti."

"Huh?" Oliver grunted.

"Djibouti!" His sister jumped to her feet, waving her arms like a lunatic and rocking the boat back and forth. "Djibouti! Djibouti! Djibouti!"

Their parents, Dr. Claire Navel and Dr. Ogden Navel, ducked out of the way of Celia's flailing arms and steadied themselves on the sides of the boat. They were world-famous adventurers and the Explorers-in-Residence at the Explorers Club in New York City, and they had learned a few things in their travels, such as how to dodge a wild boar attack and how to escape a hive of enraged killer bees. They found the same tactic came in handy when dealing with their eleven-and-a-half-year-old twins: get out of the way as quickly as possible.

Oliver fell off his narrow bench, laughing at his sister. He splashed into a puddle in the shallow hull of the boat, but he was laughing too hard to care.

He knew, of course, that Djibouti was the city whose lights were twinkling on the shore a short distance away on the coast of North Africa. He'd seen at least five episodes of his favorite spy TV show, *Agent Zero*, that were set in Djibouti.

He probably knew more about Djibouti than Celia did. He just liked hearing his sister yell it over and over again.

"What is *so* funny about Djibouti?" Celia demanded. Oliver snickered and pulled himself back up onto his bench.

Brothers can be so immature, she thought. She was three minutes and forty-two seconds older than Oliver, but sometimes it seemed like she was three years older. Oliver was giggling like an idiot just because Djibouti sounded like "booty." She noticed her father was smirking too.

Celia looked at her mother and rolled her eyes. Boys never grew up.

"It's just the city's name." She blew a strand of hair out of her face. "Djibouti."

"Bwaaah!" Oliver exploded in laughter again. He leaned over the side of the boat, turning bright red and shaking. He held his hand up in the air. "Enough," he gasped. "No more . . . I can't . . . don't say it again . . ."

"Djibouti," said Celia.

"Bwaaah!" Oliver cried, convulsing with violent laughter.

"Djibouti," she said again.

Oliver was turning purple, doubled over, long past the point when laughing was fun but unable to stop. We all certainly know the feeling, which usually occurs at the least opportune moment, such as during study hall or when a famed astronomer is giving a lecture on the ice mountains of Uranus.

"Oliver, calm down," Dr. Claire Navel, Oliver and Celia's mother, said. She grabbed Oliver by the back of his T-shirt to keep him from laughing himself over the edge of the boat. "And Celia, stop harassing your brother."

"He asked for it," said Celia.

"Be that as it may"—their mother looked from Celia to Oliver and back again—"there is nothing funny about Djibouti."

Their father snickered, but his wife shot him a glance that could have melted the ice mountains on Uranus. He fixed his face into a serious expression and stayed silent.

"The city is a den of pirates, thieves, and tourists," their mother continued. "Who knows what they're doing to poor Corey Brandt in there?"

"Don't forget Dennis," said Oliver.

Dennis was a chicken. Technically, being a male chicken, he was a rooster, but we don't really need to be so persnickety, do we?

The important thing to know about Dennis is that he was a chicken who had proven himself intelligent and heroic, in spite of having once served as bird-in-residence aboard a pirate ship. He had belonged to the captain, a ferocious rogue named Big Bart, but Bonnie, another pirate on Big Bart's crew, took Dennis the chicken prisoner at the same time that she kidnapped Corey Brandt.

Corey Brandt, we should note, was not a chicken. He was an actor. He had, however, once dressed as a chicken for a discount mattress commercial. That was a long time ago, and he doesn't like to talk about it.

Currently, Corey Brandt was the most famous teenager in the world, star of hit television shows like *Agent Zero, The Celebrity Adventurist,* and the groundbreaking teen vampire drama *Sunset High.* He wasn't yet eighteen years old, but he earned more money in a day sitting in his trailer wearing vampire fangs than the entire population of Djibouti earned in a year.

It was no wonder pirates were holding him for ransom.

Corey was also Oliver and Celia's best friend in the world, like a cool older brother, and he had been kidnapped while trying to reunite the twins with their parents and find a map to the lost city of Atlantis. The Navels were happy to be reunited. It had been years since they had all been together, but they hadn't been able to keep the map to Atlantis from falling into the hands of an evil explorer or keep Corey from falling into the hands of a vicious pirate.

It had taken weeks to track the pirates from the Pacific Ocean, through the Strait of Malacca, across the Bay of Bengal, along the Kerala coast of India, and now across the Arabian Sea to

Djibouti, and the twins were not only missing most of sixth grade, which they didn't mind one bit, they were also missing the season finales of all their favorite TV shows, which they minded quite a lot.

"Are you sure this plan will work?" Celia asked her mother. "Because I'm missing the last episode of *Celebrity Fashion Crimes*."

"And the new season of *World's Best Rodeo Clown*," said Oliver.

"And *Love at 30,000 Feet*," said Celia.

"And *Soup Wars*," said Oliver.

"And *Bizarro Bandits*," the twins said together.

They were missing a lot of television.

"We'll get you home soon," their mother told them with a sigh. She couldn't understand why they'd rather watch TV than plan a raid on a pirate stronghold in Djibouti. "The Prague Proposition is foolproof."

"But this isn't Prague," said Celia. "It's Djibouti."

"Bwah—" Oliver started to laugh, but Celia scowled at him. He clamped his hands over his mouth. Dr. Ogden Navel let out one high-pitched giggle.

"I've adapted the plan for this city," their mother said.

"So why not call it something else?" Oliver suggested. "Like the Djibouti Jinx?"

"Oh, that's good, Ollie! You're thinking like a real explorer now!" His mother licked her thumb and tried to press Oliver's stray hair flat against his head. He flinched and ducked away but couldn't help smirking just a little. He'd never admit it, but he liked that he'd impressed his mother.

"What'll happen to Corey if the Djbou—" Celia glanced at Oliver. "If the plan doesn't work?"

"You worry too much," she said. "The Prague—I mean, the Djibouti Jinx will work."

"It better." Celia glanced across the water at the city, which stuck out into the Gulf of Aden like a stray hair on Africa's head. "Or else we'll have missed all our shows for nothing."

"Trust me," their mother said, smiling at her family. She grabbed her husband's hand and squeezed it. "We're all together again. Nothing can possibly go wrong."

2
WE'RE JINXED IN DJIBOUTI

EVERYTHING WAS GOING wrong.

The stuffy storeroom behind the Saba Importing Company was too hot, and the sweat was soaking through his heavy makeup. The large gentleman could feel his face beginning to run, like a sad clown stuck out in the rain. If his disguise failed, it meant doom not just for himself, but for the Navel family, for Corey Brandt, and for one unfortunate chicken named Dennis.

"Bwak," said the chicken, who was in a cage sitting on top of a stack of imported carpets. A dim lightbulb hung from the ceiling in the center of the room, swinging slowly clockwise, casting ever-shifting shadows.

"Mrmml hurml mrrmm," said the teenager with the perfect hair, teardrop freckle under his eye, and greasy cloth in his mouth. He was tied to a metal folding chair across a wooden table from the big sweating man. Even bigger men with tattoos and knives stood guard by the door.

Next to the teenager sat the pirate captain Bonnie, a great-great-great-great-granddaughter of one of the most notorious pirates ever to sail the seas. Bonnie had taken over her ship when the previous captain was . . . how to put this politely? Forced into early retirement, perhaps?

To put it impolitely, he was murdered by Bonnie and his own crew tossed him overboard into the churning sea, where sharks made a meal of his remains.

Pirates are not known for their manners.

"You look ill." Bonnie sneered at the sweating gentleman. "Are you going to pass out? That would cause a problem for our deal."

"It's just very hot in here, that's all," the gentleman told her, forgetting himself and mopping his dripping brow with his tie.

"You've ruined your cravat," said Bonnie.

"Huh?"

Bonnie pointed at the gentleman's necktie. A blob of heavy makeup had smeared off his forehead and covered one of the cheerful ducks embroidered into the silk.

"What did you say your name was?" Bonnie

frowned at him. Two of her big associates inched closer to him, gripping their knives.

"My name . . . is . . . um, Mr. Chaterjee," the gentleman said. He wished he could stop sweating. Why had they arranged to meet in this sweltering room? He could barely breathe. He had warned Claire Navel that this plan was a bad idea. He was no good at disguises. He'd jinx the whole operation. "Aloysius B. Chaterjee, just like I told you on the telephone." He tried to sound confident.

"I think not." Bonnie squinted at him. "I've heard of another man who wears ties with ducks on them. Professor Rasmali-Greenberg, the president of the Explorers Club. He is famous for his duck ties. I do hope, for your sake, that you are not this professor in disguise."

"Is this a duck?" Professor Rasmali-Greenberg—for that's who he really was—pretended to study his tie.

"It is a duck," said Bonnie coldly.

"I thought it was a pigeon," the professor lied.

"It's a duck," said Bonnie.

"Or a moose? Maybe a lemur." He rubbed it with his thumb. "I am certain that it's a lemur."

"It is a duck," Bonnie repeated.

"Regardless, your accusation is absurd," said the professor. "I am Aloysius B. Chaterjee, a movie producer from Bombay, and I am here to buy this teenager to put him in my movies back in India."

"Mumbai," said Bonnie.

"Huh?" said the professor in disguise.

"The city is called Mumbai now, not Bombay. They changed it years ago."

"Of course." He smiled. "I am just old fashioned."

"Uh-huh." Bonnie studied him. "So, why do you want the chicken?"

"I thought you said it was a duck?"

"Not on the tie," said Bonnie. "The chicken in the cage."

Dennis clucked.

"Also for my movies," said the professor. "I am thinking of making a musical about a teenager who falls in love with a bird, who is really a princess living under a curse that transformed her into a chicken."

"This chicken is a rooster," said Bonnie. "A boy chicken."

"Well, I can put a dress on it and add eyelashes," said the professor.

"You're lying," said Bonnie.

"How do you know? Have you ever tried to attach eyelashes to a chicken?"

"No," said Bonnie. "You are lying about being a movie producer."

"I am certainly not lying," lied the professor. "I am an important producer of Bollywood films, a pioneer of Indian cinema. Now, if we could continue to move this deal along, I must get back to Mumbai to finish filming my latest picture."

"Mrmrmrmr mrmrm," groaned the teenager, squirming in his chair.

"I have the money here, in my briefcase." The professor reached for his briefcase, pouring sweat.

"Stop!" Bonnie commanded. The professor froze.

They stared at each other in silence for a time, the light still twirling above them.

"Bwak," said Dennis, breaking the tension. It is quite well known among poultry farmers that chickens cannot stand tension. It is for this reason, perhaps, that pirates do not often keep chickens as pets aboard their vessels. Piracy is fraught with tension.

"I know who you are," Bonnie said at last. "Don't deny it any longer. You are Professor

Rasmali-Greenberg, president of the Explorers Club. You have come to rescue Corey Brandt, and that is a duck on your tie!"

The professor's shoulders slumped.

"I do wish the Navels would have come themselves," Bonnie continued, "so I could get rid of you all at once, but I guess I will have to start with you alone."

"I had hoped we could do this without anyone getting hurt." The professor sighed. "You are right, of course. I am Professor Rasmali-Greenberg, president of the Explorers Club, collector of duck ties, and friend to the Navel family, but you are wrong about one thing."

"What's that?" Bonnie demanded.

"I am not alone."

The professor snapped open the clasps on his briefcase, and out leaped a very aggrieved gray howler monkey with a shock of black hair on his head and an even more aggrieved *Heloderma horridum*, also known as a bearded lizard.

For those of you who have never watched *Wally Worm's Word World*, one of Celia's favorite educational programs, you should know that *aggrieved* means a sense of having been unfairly treated. Wally Worm uses a rhyme to remember it: *If ever you are not believed, don't feel angry, feel aggrieved.*

The aggrieved lizard was named Beverly, and she was aggrieved because she had just spent three hours squished into a briefcase with a howler monkey. The monkey's name was Patrick, and he didn't enjoy his time in the briefcase either.

For those of you who have never been attacked by an aggrieved lizard or howler monkey, I do not recommend it, and I do not think that Bonnie and her pirate thugs would recommend it either. The beaded lizard has a venomous bite that is quite unpleasant, causing convulsions, vomiting, unconsciousness, and, in some cases, death. Oddly, for those who do survive, lima beans taste much better.

The howler monkey just has very sharp teeth, which he does not hesitate to use.

As soon as Beverly and Patrick leaped, hissing and howling, from the briefcase, Beverly chomped on the ankle of one of Bonnie's thugs, who shouted and cursed in Mandarin Chinese. Then he fell unconscious. Patrick knocked the knife from another pirate's hands and bit him hard on the wrist. The words the pirate shrieked were unclear, either because they were in Norwegian or because the monkey was also choking him with its tail.

Professor Rasmali-Greenberg shot to his feet and dove across the table, knocking Corey away from the blade of Bonnie's knife. The chair toppled over backward and the large Explorers Club president landed on top of the teenage celebrity with a bone-crushing thud.

"I hot orby ant," the young man moaned through the gag in his mouth and promptly passed out.

Bonnie was on her feet, knife in hand, preparing to throw it into the professor's back, when Beverly hopped onto the table in front of her.

"Hiss!" said the beaded lizard.

"Aieee!!!" said Bonnie, dropping her knife and running from the room. Not one of her unfortunate guards was still standing, and it was doubtful that any of them would be able to stand for some time.

"Well, it wasn't pretty," said Professor Rasmali-Greenberg as he scooped Corey's limp body up and tossed the teen over his shoulder. "But we got what we came for."

"Bwak," added Dennis the chicken.

The professor picked up Dennis's cage and

slipped out of the Saba Importing Company store-room with Corey Brandt still unconscious over his shoulder. Patrick the monkey and Beverly the lizard followed close behind. The small band kept to the back streets and dark alleys, weaving their way through the Djibouti night.

Neither man nor lizard nor monkey nor chicken noticed that a small figure with thick scars on his forehead scurried behind them, following from the shadows.

3
WE RERUN

"WHAT HAPPENED TO Corey?" Celia cried, rushing across the beach to meet Professor Rasmali-Greenberg as the sun rose over the ocean.

The professor set the teenager down on the sand and then let Dennis the chicken out of his cage. Patrick and Beverly watched Dennis closely, no doubt considering whether he was a friend or a meal.

"Things did not go quite as planned," the professor told the Navels as he wiped the rest of his runny makeup off with a handkerchief.

"But the Prague Proposition is foolproof," objected Claire Navel.

"You mean the Djibouti Jinx," said Oliver. He turned to the professor. "I renamed it."

"*We* renamed it," corrected Celia, kneeling down to check if Corey was still breathing. She was the teenager's biggest fan, after all, and felt a certain duty toward him.

Oliver rolled his eyes. *Access Celebrity Tonight* called Corey Brandt a teen heartthrob. Oliver imagined that a heartthrob was a serious medical problem. It didn't seem to bother Celia that Corey might be a serious medical problem. His sister always got weird around him. Maybe she needed to see a doctor.

"Your plan may have been foolproof," the professor told them, "but it was not pirate proof. Bonnie saw right through my disguise. Things got out of control. Bonnie escaped, young Mr. Brandt was knocked out, and I ruined one of my favorite ties."

"No!" Celia popped up and backed away from the unconscious celebrity.

"I'm afraid so," said the professor. "You can see for yourself that the tie is ruined. Makeup stains right across the embroidery."

"No," said Celia. "I mean, Corey Brandt was *not* knocked out."

"Celia, honey," her father said, putting his hand on her shoulder, "he was knocked out. Look. He's right in front of you. Have you been drinking enough water? Too much water? In fact, we aren't supposed to drink the water here because of toxic parasites." He turned to his wife. "I think Celia has toxic parasites."

"I don't have toxic parasites," said Celia. She pointed at the unconscious celebrity. "*That's* not Corey Brandt."

Oliver kneeled down to get a closer look. He wiped his thumb under Corey's eye.

"Oh man!" he groaned. He raised his thumb to show his parents the black smudge. Corey's teardrop freckle was gone. "It's Ernest," Oliver said sadly. "Again."

"That sneaky, lying, no-good pirate," said the professor. "She tricked me!"

"I can't believe you fell for that," said Celia.

"Again," added Oliver.

"I feel like we're stuck in a rerun!" Celia shook her head.

Ernest was a celebrity impersonator. He had pretended to be Corey Brandt before. He was voted off of *Dancing with My Impersonator* for his bad impression of Corey Brandt (he was too old) and his even worse dancing (he couldn't waltz). His impression of the teenager got better, though, because he had tricked the Navels into going with him to the Amazon, pretending he was Corey Brandt the whole time, until they figured it out and he tried to kill them.

He had tried to kill them a few times since then too, but not dressed as Corey Brandt. Every time they thought they had escaped him, he turned up, just like a bad case of the hiccups.

Up close he looked way too old to be a teenager. On TV, older people played teenagers all the time, but in real life, Celia and Oliver could tell the difference. They were pretty upset that Professor Rasmali-Greenberg couldn't.

"Young people all look the same to me," the professor explained.

"Well," Dr. Navel—their father—said. "This is a problem."

"Yeah," Dr. Navel—their mother—agreed. "We need to find the real Corey Brandt and get out of Djibouti. Sir Edmund will probably be on his way to Atlantis by now."

The twins gave each other a nervous look, just like they did whenever someone mentioned Sir Edmund. He was a ruthless billionaire explorer who had pursued them all over the world, from the high mountaintops of Tibet through the Amazon and to a remote island in the South Pacific.

As far as enemies went, he was even worse than a celebrity impersonator or a vicious pirate. He kept a private zoo for rare, dangerous, and mythical creatures. His breath smelled worse than a sandwich abandoned at the bottom of a school locker for six months. He wanted to find Atlantis because he thought he could raise it from the depths of the ocean and rule the world. He was a very little man with a very big mustache and an even bigger ego.

While their mother was determined to stop him from finding Atlantis, Oliver and Celia were determined not to get thrown out of any more airplanes or chased through any more jungles or forced to battle any more giant squid. They just wanted a normal life, like normal kids, even if that meant that they had to go back to sixth grade.

Of course, first they had to rescue their friend from the pirates in Djibouti, which was hardly a normal thing for a sixth grader to do.

"Ugh," Ernest groaned, slowly coming to.

"You!" Celia shouted at him.

His eyes snapped open. "Huh? What? Navels!"

"That's right," said Oliver.

"Oh thank you!" Ernest pushed himself off the sand and threw himself at Oliver and Celia's feet. "I'm so glad to see you! I can't take it any longer . . . the pirates are terrible. They beat me and mocked me and make me waltz for their amusement."

"You can't waltz!" said Celia.

"I know." Ernest wept. "I hoped you'd come to save me. I prayed you'd come!"

"We didn't come for *you*," Celia sneered at him. "We came for Corey Brandt."

"Oh." Ernest looked down at his clothes and slumped back onto his knees. "Right." He sighed and looked at Claire and Ogden Navel. "But you could take me with you, right? I promise I won't cause any trouble. Just don't make me go back to those pirates."

"We would never do that," said Ogden Navel.

"Well," his wife shrugged, "I wouldn't say *never . . .*"

Ernest dove onto his face, groveling at her feet. "Mrs. Navel, please! I'll do anything!"

"It's *Doctor* Navel," she corrected. "I had my PhD before my husband did."

"I don't test well." Dr. Navel blushed.

"Doctor Navel, *Doctors* Navel!" Ernest whined, writhing on the ground like an agitated eel. "Pleeease!"

"You have to promise not to disguise yourself again or betray us in any way," said Claire Navel.

"I promise," said Ernest.

"And you cannot, under any circumstances, try to kill my children," she added.

"Again," grumbled Celia.

"Of course not!" Ernest pushed himself off the ground. He looked at Oliver and Celia with wide, wet eyes. "I'm sorry, Oliver. I'm sorry, Celia. I never should have tried to kill you. I fell in with a bad crowd. Sir Edmund and his Council and his grave robber accomplices. They made me do it. I would never want to hurt children."

"Lying snake," Oliver snapped at him.

"And we're tweens, not children," Celia added. She turned to her mother. "Mom, you can't be serious about helping him."

Ernest looked back and forth between mother and daughter, whimpering like a sad puppy.

"Can it!" Celia shouted at him. Ernest stopped whimpering.

"We'll be turning him over to the police as soon as possible," Claire Navel told her daughter. "And you"—she narrowed her eyes at Ernest—"you will confess everything. Kidnapping, attempted murder, identity theft."

"Don't forget destruction of property!" Professor Rasmali-Greenberg added. "I hold him personally responsible for ruining my tie!"

"But—" Ernest objected.

Claire held her hand in the air and gave him that look that only mothers, teachers, and dictators of small Latin American countries can give. Ernest fell silent.

"You will also tell us where the real Corey Brandt is being held," she added.

"He's in one of the pirates' desert strongholds outside the city," said Ernest.

"Why would pirates be in the desert?" Celia scoffed. "He's lying. We should look for their ship."

"I'm not lying. I can draw you a map to the place. The pirates only use their ship to stage attacks," Ernest said. "They are normally based on land, outside the city, where the corrupt local governor gives them protection."

"Protection from what?" Oliver wondered. Why would pirates need protection from a governor?

"From the law," said Ernest. "And from people like you."

Oliver puffed his chest up a little. He liked the idea of pirates needing protection from him. Celia rolled her eyes and Oliver deflated again.

"So how are we supposed to get them?" Oliver wondered.

Claire and Ogden Navel gave each other a quick glance and a nod.

"It will be very dangerous to invade a pirate stronghold," their mother told them. "I know you two have faced danger before, but someone will need to guard Ernest. The professor, your father, Patrick, and I can take care of the rescue operation at first light, when the pirates will still be asleep."

"Pirates are not morning people," the professor explained.

"Exactly," said Claire Navel. "So I think we'll get a hotel room. Oliver and Celia will take

Beverly and Dennis and our prisoner and stay behind to—"

"Okay," the twins said in unison. They didn't need to be convinced to stay in a hotel while their parents took care of the dangerous adventures. Maybe they'd get lucky and there would be a TV in the hotel room; maybe it would have cable.

It was about time they got to relax while somebody else saved the day.

4

WE CHECK IN

"THIS HOTEL IS gross," Oliver muttered. "It smells like Sir Edmund's breath."

He sat on the edge of a small metal bed, looking around at the grimy hotel room. Strange stains spread on the tattered rug. Bugs buzzed this way and that. No wonder they were the only guests. This was not the sort of place that the Travel Channel would recommend. This was not the sort of place that the Health and Wellness Channel would recommend either.

Beverly, being a poisonous lizard, quite liked the hotel room for the exact same reasons Oliver thought it was gross. She scurried to and fro along the floor and up the walls, gobbling up beetles and flies and mosquitoes. Oliver cringed with every crunch. He found lizards very unsettling.

"We have to keep a low profile," said Celia.

"It's not like we could just check into the nicest hotel in town. We have a prisoner."

She nodded to Ernest, who was tied up and gagged. Their parents had dumped him on the other metal bed, face down so that any complaining he did through his gag was muffled by the pillows. Dennis had decided to pace back and forth over the prisoner's back, his little chicken claws scratching Ernest mercilessly. Ernest groaned but didn't struggle. It seemed only fair that he should be a little uncomfortable after all the times he'd tried to murder Oliver and Celia.

"Anyway," said Celia. "At least we have something to do while we wait for Mom and Dad to get back with Corey." She ran her hand along an old television sitting on a stand. A cloud of dust billowed. She coughed.

"But there's no remote," Oliver complained.

Oliver never remembered anything, thought Celia. She crossed the room and rummaged in her backpack, pushing aside some wetsuits, an old leather journal that had once belonged to the long-lost explorer Percy Fawcett, a brass compass with Percy Fawcett's initials on it, some empty snack cake wrappers, and a few empty cheese puff bags, until she found their big universal remote control.

It had seen better days.

There were two buttons missing, although they were buttons the twins never knew what to do with anyway. There were nuclear-orange stains around the channel changer from cheese puff dust, and a dried crust of salt from when Oliver had dropped into it an underwater cave. The remote had been through a lot with them. But it had also been blessed by a monk in Tibet, and now it could work on any TV in the world. The remote also had a few other unique abilities, but the twins didn't care so much about those right now. They just wanted to watch TV.

Celia pointed the remote at the television, closed her eyes, and pressed the power button. She waited. She opened one eye, cocked her head, and smiled!

"It worked!"

"It did?" said Oliver. The screen looked just as dark as it had before.

"Listen," said Celia.

They listened. A quiet hum grew louder and louder; the darkness on the screen lightened to gray, then to a lighter gray, then to white and gray.

"See?" said Celia. "These old TVs just have to warm up. In the old days, people had to wait for, like, a whole minute while their TVs got started."

"That's horrible."

"I know," said Celia. "Let's see if we get any channels." She hit the channel-changer button. More static. She hit it again. Static, static, and more static.

"Bo-ring," said Oliver.

He threw himself backward onto the bed, forgetting how gross he thought it was. He was tired and really wanted to watch TV, even if it was one of the dumb soap operas that Celia always made him watch, like *Love at 30,000 Feet*. As long as it wasn't one of those fashion shows.

"Ooh, *Celebrity Fashion Crimes* is on!" Celia squealed.

"Anything but that!" Oliver groaned. *Celebrity Fashion Crimes* was about celebrities in terrible outfits giving free makeovers to non-famous people who looked fine until the celebrities came along. "Can't we look for *Agent Zero*?"

"No," said Celia. She'd had enough action and adventure for a while.

"How about *Bizarro Bandits*?" Oliver suggested.

"We're watching TV in a filthy hotel with a lizard, a chicken, and an evil celebrity impersonator while our parents, a professor, and a monkey try to rescue an actual celebrity from pirates," said Celia. "Things are bizarre enough already."

"What about *Soup Wars*?" Oliver loved cooking shows.

"It's too hot for soup," said Celia.

"*World's Best Rodeo Clown*?"

"We're watching *Celebrity Fashion Crimes*."

"Oh come on! Let's just look for *World's Best Rodeo Clown*!"

"*Celebrity Fashion Crimes*. That's final."

"Ugh," said Oliver.

"Hiss," said Beverly.

Celia gave them both a look that silenced them. She had her mother's gift for it. Sometimes, she thought, both brothers and poisonous lizards needed to be reminded who was the boss. She was three minutes and forty-two seconds older, after all.

On TV, Madam Mumu, the pop star of all pop stars, was in a canoe with a sad-faced girl in a pretty sundress. The girl was holding a fishing line and looking glum.

"You need carp!" Madam Mumu shouted. *"A freshwater fish is the fashion-forward way to a fancy hat!"*

"Bo-ring!" Oliver groaned.

"You'll have to stay in cooler climates so the hat doesn't start to smell," Madam Mumu was telling the girl. *"How do you feel about moving to the arctic archipelago of Svalbard? It's cold, but you get to see the wonder of the aurora borealis glowing in the twilight sky. Some of the ice sheets off the coast are thousands of years old. They're as thick as skyscrapers! Your outfit will really pop against that background. You'll love it!"*

The girl on screen did not look like she would love it.

"Now let's get back to your campsite!" said Madam Mumu. *"After this commercial break, we'll make a dress out of your tent! It's warm, fireproof, and almost indestructible!"*

"Boring, boring, boring, boring, boring," said Oliver.

"Stop it," said Celia.

"Boring, boring, boring, boring, boring."

"Shh."

"Boring, boring, boring, boring, boring."

Celia turned up the volume to drown out her brother.

For those readers who do not yet know Celia and Oliver very well, you may wonder how they can focus so much on television under their current circumstances. You see, while some children might have been filled with anxiety about guarding a prisoner while their parents staged the daring rescue of a celebrity from a pirate stronghold in the desert outside Djibouti, Oliver and Celia were not so easily impressed.

Danger was nothing new to them—they'd been facing danger since before they could walk. Distant lands were about as interesting for these two as folding socks. And they were certainly used to their parents running off on one foolish quest or another.

Their mother had run off when they were eight years old to search for the Lost Library of Alexandria. After three years without a word from her, she had suddenly reappeared on a mountaintop in Tibet. She told the twins that she loved them and missed them—all that normal mother stuff—and then she told them that she was part of an ancient secret society called the Mnemones, the scribes of the Lost Library of Alexandria back before it became lost. The *M* in Mnemones is silent, just like the *D* in Djibouti.

Being an explorer, we should note, involves lots of silent letters and secret societies.

Their mother also told Oliver and Celia that they were the last of the Mnemones and that they had to find the Lost Library of Alexandria before Sir Edmund did or the whole world was doomed. Then she disappeared again without so much as a bedtime story.

She showed up a few months after that in the Amazon, and then again on a desert island in the Pacific Ocean, always talking about her secret society and the fate of the world and Oliver and Celia's destiny.

Of course, every time she showed up, the twins' lives were in danger. It was unclear whether she showed up to protect them or if she brought the danger with her.

Either way, because of her quest for the Lost Library, Celia and Oliver had battled monstrous yetis in Tibet, biting fire ants in the Amazon, giant squid on the Pacific Ocean, and faced witches, warriors, goons, and grave robbers. They'd ridden a yak, escaped crumbling ruins and an erupting volcano, and watched their favorite actor get kidnapped by pirates. They'd also been thrown out of an airplane.

That one, their mother confessed, had been her fault.

At least on TV the adventures came with special effects and the story was neatly tied up after half an hour. Even better, the twins didn't have to go anywhere or do anything to have TV adventures. Excitement, they had long ago decided, was more exciting when it was happening to someone else.

"You know when Mom and Dad get back they'll want us to go with them on another adventure, right?" Oliver said, staring up at the ceiling.

Celia didn't answer. She knew her brother was right, and she hated when that happened.

"They'll want us to go looking for Atlantis," he continued. "That's where Mom thinks the Lost Library is hidden."

"That *is* where it is hidden," Celia told her brother. She'd found Percy Fawcett's journal that said so.

"We'll have to beat Sir Edmund there," Oliver added.

"Of course, when in Svalbard, you must watch out for walruses," Madam Mumu continued to lecture the girl on TV. "Polar bears are obviously best avoided, but an angry walrus can be equally dangerous. They are a status-driven species, so it is important to establish a dominant posture."

"We could . . . you know." Oliver hesitated. He worried that his sister was going to yell at him for what he was about to suggest. She was pretty good at establishing a dominant posture and she always got the final say on what they watched on TV or who went first into ancient ruins. "We could help them," he said. "Mom and Dad are pretty hopeless without us."

Celia sat on the edge of the bed and stared straight at the TV. Of course they could help their parents, she thought. In spite of themselves, they'd become pretty good adventurers.

Oliver pulled the old leather journal from the bag and flipped through it. There was a lot of faded writing and drawings from the old explorer's travels. Some pages were filled from edge to edge with tiny words, others had sketches of the fabled city of Atlantis, with a large temple in the center and rings of walls and moats stretching out from it like ripples in a pond. A statue of

Poseidon, Greek god of the sea, stood at the entrance to its vast gates.

Other pages had odd symbols and crazy drawings of monsters like yetis and giant squid, unicorns and dragons. There was, for some reason, a whole page with a picture of a buck-toothed squirrel arguing with an old bearded man. The explorer who kept this journal must have gone crazy when he vanished in the jungle. What sort of adult would draw a picture of a man arguing with a squirrel?

The back page of the journal was filled with pictures of a tree. Not different trees. Just one big tree—the same tree—over and over again.

"C-r-a-z-y," Oliver muttered. He got bored and threw the journal back into the bag. "I mean, if we helped Mom and Dad, we wouldn't have to go back to sixth grade yet," he finally said. "And we do have that remote control. It could help."

Celia studied the remote in her hands. It wasn't just a universal remote control. It also had the ability to access the complete catalog of the Lost Library of Alexandria from any TV anywhere in the world.

I know what you're thinking.

Big deal, right? It's just a library catalog.

Well, no one actually knows everything the Lost Library contained in its collections. It was destroyed two thousand years ago in a terrible fire, and all its contents were believed lost. Except they were not lost. They were rescued from destruction and hidden away, maps of forgotten civilizations—like Atlantis—along with scrolls of ancient wisdom and power, magic and intrigue, accounting records and instruction manuals.

Those last two don't sound so exciting, but the accounting records document all the wealth of the ancient world, and the instruction manuals might just show how to raise the lost city of Atlantis. For that reason, the rich and powerful have long sought to find and control the library. And for that same reason, the Mnemones have been trying to find it first.

"And anyway, the sooner we help Mom and Dad find Atlantis and get to the Lost Library, the sooner we can all go home," Oliver added.

"Fine," Celia said. "We'll help Mom and Dad. But just this one time," she added. "Then we get to go home and watch TV and never have another adventure again. Agreed?"

"Agreed," said Oliver. "Now, gimme the remote."

"*Celebrity Fashion Crimes* isn't over yet."

"But you just said we could use the remote to help Mom and Dad."

"After *Celebrity Fashion Crimes.*"

"No," Oliver whined.

"Just a minute!"

"Come on!" Oliver dove for the remote and Celia tried to pull it away.

"No!" she yelled as he tugged at it and she tugged back. They pulled and twisted and wrestled and pushed over the remote control while Dennis and Beverly watched from Ernest's back.

"Give it!" grunted Oliver.

"You'll break it!" grunted Celia.

"Will not!"

"Will too!"

"Will—oh." Oliver stopped struggling and Celia snatched the remote back from him. She followed his eyes to the TV screen and saw that they were no longer watching *Celebrity Fashion Crimes.*

Instead, they were looking at an entry in the catalog of the Lost Library of Alexandria.

"*The Life and Voyages of Saint Nicholas of Myra,*" Celia read aloud. "Fourth century AD, three scrolls in his own hand."

"What's that supposed to mean?" said Oliver.

"It means that the library had three scrolls written by Saint Nicholas of Myra in the fourth century."

"When was that?"

"A long time ago."

"Where's Myra?"

"Beats me."

"Who was Saint Nicholas?"

Celia shrugged.

"Is he, like, Santa Claus?"

Celia looked sideways at her brother.

"You know," said Oliver. "Like Old Saint Nick?"

"Don't be such a baby," said Celia. "There's no such thing as Santa Claus."

"How would you know?" said Oliver.

"Because," said Celia, "I'm older."

"We're twins!"

"I'm still older."

"By three minutes!"

"And forty-two seconds," she added. "Anyway, what would Santa Claus have to do with the Lost Library?"

That one stumped Oliver.

"See?" said Celia. "He's not real."

"He could be real," Oliver grumbled.

"Could not," said Celia.

"Could too," said Oliver.

"Could not."

"Could too."

Although their argument was of the utmost seriousness, Oliver and Celia actually quite enjoyed arguing with each other and could have happily debated the existence of Santa Claus for hours, if, at that moment, their parents, Professor Rasmali-Greenberg, Patrick the monkey, and the real Corey Brandt had not burst through the door, out of breath.

"Oliver, Celia!" Their father rushed across the room. "We've got to go, right now!"

"But we were just about to—" Oliver had just pointed back at the screen when he heard the unmistakable shouts of an angry mob growing nearer. Explorers—and the children of explorers—learn from a very young age what the shouts of an angry mob sound like—a bit like the ocean in a seashell, a bit like a handful of forks tossed into a blender.

In this case, a very big blender and a whole lot of forks.

5

WE MAKE A LONG STORY SHORT

"HEY GUYS." COREY nodded at Oliver and Celia as he slammed the door behind him and leaned against it. He had a bruise next to his left eye, just to the side of his teardrop freckle, and his perfect hair was long and greasy and not at all perfect. His clothes were tattered. "I guess I'm doing a whole, like, retro-grunge look, huh?" He smiled widely.

"So retro," Celia said, not really knowing what he meant but liking the way he smiled when he said it.

Oliver rolled his eyes, but Celia elbowed him in the side. Corey gave Oliver a high-five, which he happily accepted.

"So, did the pirates torture you?" Oliver asked.

"Only on the first day." Corey shrugged. "An argument broke out about the series finale of

Sunset High and, well, they settled it with fists. Team Annabel and Team Lauren took out their disagreements on my face. Who knew that pirates cared so much about romance? But after that was settled, they were pretty decent. My hand got sore from signing autographs and scrubbing floors, but otherwise—"

"There's no time!" Dr. Navel cut him off and pulled Ernest up from the bed.

"Mrrrmmm," Ernest groaned.

"We're not, like, taking him with us, are we?" Corey asked.

"We made a promise," said Dr. Navel.

"We'll turn him over to the authorities once we've escaped the angry mob," said their mother.

"Bwak!" squawked Dennis.

"So, uh, why is there an angry mob chasing you?" Oliver wondered.

"You don't need to say angry mob," said Celia. "You can just say mob. All mobs are angry."

"Whatever," said Oliver. "Why is there a mob after you?"

"The rescue didn't go all that smoothly," their mother explained. "Patrick snuck into the pirate stronghold and located Corey Brandt, just like he was supposed to."

The monkey clapped for himself.

"The pirates were running around, packing things up to leave," their mother continued. "Bonnie was furious that the professor had escaped and she was preparing a search party to go after him."

"She imagined that I would fetch a nice ransom." Professor Rasmali-Greenberg smiled. "As president of the Explorers Club, I do have many wealthy friends. The royal family of Monaco attended my last birthday party."

"Uh-huh." Oliver and Celia shrugged, unimpressed.

"Anyway," said their mother. "To make a long story short—"

"Too late," said the twins in unison.

"The professor created a distraction while your father and I took Corey."

"They kept me chained to a post outside!" the teenager added. "Check out my tan! And my scorpion bites!"

He seemed pretty excited about his tan and his scorpion bites. Celia was afraid he'd gone crazy, but it was very hard to tell with celebrities, and even harder to tell with teenage boys.

"Anyway, we were making our way out of the camp when—," their mother said.

"There's a window back here." Dr. Navel ran in from the bathroom. "We can climb out that way and escape the angry mob."

"You don't need to say angry," repeated Celia.

"Honey," said their mother, smiling way too politely, "I am trying to tell the story about why the mob is chasing us in the first place."

"But honey," Dr. Navel said, smiling back, "the mob is going to tear us apart any minute."

"Yes, honey." Claire smiled back at her husband. "Don't you think the kids would like to know *why* the mob is going to tear them apart?"

"I don't think they do, darling," said Dr. Navel. "I think they'd prefer to escape without being torn apart."

"But it's a really good story, sweetheart," she answered him.

"I am sure they'd love to hear it later, dear."

"It won't be as interesting later, dear."

"I think it will be interesting later, dear."

"I think it won't."

"It will."

"It won't."

"It will."

"It won't."

"It will—oh, never mind." Dr. Navel threw his hands in the air. "Finish the story then. If we're still alive when this mob of goat herders tears us limb from limb, then we'll make our escape."

"Ogden!" Claire Navel shook her head. "You just ruined the end of the story. The goat herders were the best part. Now I don't even want to tell it."

Just then, a large bottle with a flaming rag sticking out the top of it smashed through the window and crashed into the television, where it burst into flames.

Outside, the mob roared.

"They seem really angry," said Oliver. "I think we can go back to calling them an angry mob."

"Yeah," agreed Celia as she shoved the remote control back into their backpack and handed it to her brother, who put it on without complaint as the wall behind the television caught fire. "Now, can we please make our escape?"

Her parents nodded. There was no arguing with an angry mob, a wall of fire, or Celia Navel.

6

WE HEAR HERDERS

ONE BY ONE, the band of explorers, tweens, the celebrity, the imprisoned celebrity impersonator, and the odd assortment of animals squeezed through the tiny bathroom window at the back of the hotel. Clouds of black smoke belched out around them.

One by one, they landed, coughing, in a dusty alleyway. Corey shoved Ernest, still tied up, ahead of him out the window, so his impersonator landed face first on the ground with a thump. Beverly scurried out along the wall, Patrick jumped, and Dennis flapped his useless wings, dropping through the air in a flurry of smoke and feathers.

Lastly, Professor Rasmali-Greenberg squeezed his considerable bulk through the small opening, dropped to the ground, stumbled, dusted himself off, and smiled.

"So," he said. "Shall we hail a taxi?"

"I think, like, we better just run for it," Corey suggested. "That mob is A-N-G-R-Y."

Celia narrowed her eyes at him but didn't say anything.

"We can't go that way." She pointed toward the far end of the alley, where a few stragglers from the angry mob passed by. Everyone ducked behind some old crates. Dr. Navel peeked his head out to check if they had been noticed.

"Why did you guys make all these goat herders so angry?" Oliver whispered.

"It wasn't on purpose," Corey whispered back. "The professor tried to create a distraction by letting loose a herd of goats. The goat herder got angry and started shouting. The pirates weren't far behind us, so we had to borrow the goat herder's pickup truck."

"You *stole* it?"

"Borrowed," Corey said. "We were being chased by angry pirates and an angry goat herder. Anyway, it turned out that the truck belonged to the goat herder's brother, who also started chasing us, and he has a lot of sons, so they joined in, and pretty soon, they ran into the pirates. Pirates and goat herders don't usually get along. The goat herders make an honest living and the pirates kidnap people. So they started fighting. That's when your father made a wrong turn—"

"Shh," Dr. Navel called. "Someone's coming!"

They fell silent and waited as a few stray goats ambled past the alley, joining their herders in the mob.

"Anyway," Corey whispered. "After your father turned down the wrong road, we decided we needed to take a shortcut to get back to the city, so there was this field where another herd of goats were grazing. We had no choice but to cut across it, which upset those goats and those goat herders, so they joined the chase—"

"Guys," said Celia.

"Well," Corey continued, "they started calling everyone they knew—it turns out they all have cell phones—and pretty soon there was an entire mob of angry goat herders after us."

"What happened to the pirates?" Oliver wondered.

"Guys?" said Celia.

"I don't know what happened to the pirates," said Corey. "I guess the goat herders took care of them."

"They didn't!" yelled Celia.

Everyone turned to look at her and then to look at the other end of the alley behind them, where she was pointing.

There stood Bonnie with five more of her pirate goons, blocking their way out.

"How nice to see you all again," Bonnie sneered.

"Aha!" someone yelled from the other end of the alley. Oliver and Celia spun around to see the goat herders gathering at that end, filing into the narrow space next to the burning hotel. The angry goat herders were wielding clubs and machetes and sticks. So were the pirates.

"Now what?" Oliver groaned, seeing that they were trapped between two armed groups and a burning building.

Celia found herself wondering what the other sixth graders at her school were up to at the moment. She would have happily traded places with any of them, even if they were taking a test or giving a report or climbing a rope in gym class.

She stopped herself. That was crazy thinking. Nothing could be worse than climbing a rope in gym class.

"This way," a voice called to them from the

roof on the building on the other side of the alley. A rope dropped down next to them.

In storytelling, there is a trick some writers use called *deus ex machina*. It is a Latin phrase that means "a god from the machine," and writers use it to get characters out of impossible situations by bringing in a new character or idea that comes from nowhere and saves the day. In ancient plays, the writer would actually have a god lowered onto the stage by a crane to solve all the characters' problems. The god actually came from the machine.

At this moment, the closest the Navels had to their own *deus ex machina* was a boy about Oliver and Celia's age, who was standing above them on the opposite rooftop holding onto a rope. He was dressed in rags, his skin dark against the bright blue sky, and he had three thick scars in straight lines across his forehead.

"Oh man," Celia whined, staring at the rope.

"Scarification," Dr. Navel whispered, staring at the boy. "The marks of maturity in the Dinka tribe of Sudan."

"The what tribe?" Oliver wondered.

"The Dinka are a Nilotic cow-herding people

of the Bahr al-Ghazal region," Professor Rasmali-Greenberg said.

"No-what-ic cow people of where?" Oliver wondered.

"The Bahr al-Ghazal is in south Sudan," the professor answered. "It is largely inhabited by—"

"Can we skip the educational programming and get out of here?" Celia pleaded.

"Hurry!" the boy on the roof called down.

"Just like gym class," Celia muttered as she grabbed onto the rope. More ropes dropped down and two more boys appeared next to them, smiling.

"This is the worst," Oliver groaned as he started hauling himself up, hand over hand, beside his sister.

"Use your legs more and your arms won't get tired," Celia told him.

"So you're a gym teacher now?" he muttered.

"Fine, do it your way, but when your arms turn into floppy noodles and you fall back into the alley and the angry goat herders tear you limb from limb, don't whine to me about it."

"I won't," said Oliver.

"Good," said Celia.

"Whatever," said Oliver.

Beverly scurried up the wall as Patrick raced ahead of the twins. The adults grabbed on and started climbing.

Corey climbed up after the Navels with Dennis clucking and gripping his hair.

"Ow, stop scratching me!" Corey complained.

Professor Rasmali-Greenberg lashed a rope around Ernest's ankles and then made his way up the ropes himself, grunting and pouring sweat.

"Ooph, ooph," grunted Ernest as the boys on the roof pulled his rope taut and hauled him up the wall upside down, banging and scraping him along the rough stone as they went.

"Stop them!" shouted Bonnie from below.

Her thugs charged forward. The mob of goat herders charged at the same time, but the pirates and the goat herders stopped short when a heavy spear slammed into the ground between them.

A group of full-grown Dinka warriors, each at least seven feet tall, stood next to the boys with the ropes.

"Cow herders?" Celia called down to her parents, who were climbing below her.

"The Dinka are also legendary warriors," her mother added.

"Do you think Mom knows these guys?" Oliver asked.

"I dunno," said Celia.

"I hope they're friendly," whispered Oliver, squinting up at the large men towering above the alleyway.

Down below, the goat herders and the pirates cursed at each other in a variety of languages, but no one dared to attack as long as the warriors with the spears stood poised above them.

"Just keep climbing," Celia urged her brother, because she did not want to think what would happen if these Dinka warriors turned out to be unfriendly.

7

WE'RE PRIVY TO THE PROPHECY

"COREY BRANDT!" THE Dinka boys had finished dragging Ernest up the wall and pulled the gag out of his mouth. They poked and prodded at him. "We are big fans! Big fans! Although you should have chosen Lauren at the end of *Sunset High*."

"Hey," the real Corey Brandt objected, pulling the chicken off his head. The boys looked back and forth between Ernest and Corey, puzzled. "I'm Corey Brandt!"

The boys shrugged, shoved the gag back into Ernest's mouth, and ran over to poke and prod and question the real Corey Brandt. He nodded and smiled and gave vague answers, glad to find his fans even in this remote corner of Djibouti.

"Excuse me." Dr. Navel approached one of the

tall warriors, opening his arms wide to show that his intentions were friendly. The warrior took a step backward, wary of a hug from the strange explorer whose glasses were sliding off his nose. "I'm Dr. Ogden Navel and this is my wife, Dr. Claire Navel. We are the Explorers-in-Residence at the Explorers Club in New York City. This man"—he pointed at the professor—"is Professor Rasmali-Greenberg, club president. I want to thank you for your assistance."

"Yes." The warrior nodded, keeping his spear pointed at the alley below. "We know who you are."

"You do?" Dr. Navel was puzzled. He looked to his wife.

"Don't ask me," she said. "I don't know them."

"We know who *they* are." One of the boys pointed at Oliver and Celia.

"You do?" Oliver asked.

"You are Oliver and Celia Navel," said the boy. "And you are known throughout the world for your daring exploits."

"Exploits?" Oliver shook his head.

"Daring?" asked their parents.

"Is this *Bizarro Bandits*?" Celia wondered.

On *Bizarro Bandits* a team of pranksters sneak

into people's houses in the middle of the night and did things like change the furniture and shrink all their clothes and dye their pets green, so when the people woke up they believed they were in some bizarro world. More than one contestant had gone totally insane. Those who didn't go insane won a vacation or a new toaster.

Celia was not interested in a vacation or a new toaster. Oliver was looking around for hidden cameras.

"Who are you?" asked Oliver

"How did you know we'd be here?" asked Celia.

"Your friend told us." The boy shrugged.

"Our friend?" Celia cocked her head to the side like a confused puppy.

She and Oliver didn't have a lot of friends in the sixth grade. Their father had pulled them out of school to go on adventures for most of the school year, and when they were in school, most of the kids only talked to them because they knew Corey Brandt. Celia didn't expect any of the squeaky girls who had Corey's face on their notebooks to know any Dinka warriors, and Oliver was pretty sure that none of the boys in his class had ever been to the Bahr al-Ghazal region of southern Sudan. Most of them weren't even allowed to ride the subway alone.

"Celia!" A girl dressed in a flowing white tunic with a colorful cloth bag over her shoulder climbed up on the other side of the roof.

Celia broke into a smile when she saw the girl. She wasn't a Dinka warrior and she wasn't from Oliver and Celia's school either.

"Qui!" Celia smiled at her old friend from the Amazon, whose whole name was Quinuama, but she let people call her Qui to make it easier for them. She was thoughtful that way, even though she quite liked her full name. Qui had helped Oliver and Celia find the lost city of El Dorado in the Amazon and she was their first real friend in the world. Celia had no idea how Qui had gotten all the way to North Africa, or why.

Celia ran across the roof and gave her a hug. Friends, we should note, never start by asking why.

Oliver interrupted the hug. "What are you doing here? How do you know these warriors?"

"We met on the Internet," Qui answered him with a shrug.

"The Internet?" Oliver and Celia asked.

"We use it all the time," said Qui. "We indigenous peoples have to stick together."

"Indigenous?" Oliver looked at his sister.

"You know that one," she said.

"Like native?" said Oliver. Celia nodded.

"My people are facing many of the problems the Dinka and other tribes are facing," said Qui. "From pollution and the destruction of our cultures to getting into a good college when you've lived your whole life in the jungle."

"Or in the desert," said the Dinka boy.

"Right," said Qui. "It's hard being an indigenous kid these days. So we have Internet forums and stuff. That's where I met these guys." She pointed to the Dinka warriors.

"And where I learned about your prophecy," the boy said. *"The greatest explorers shall be the least. The old ways shall come to nothing, while new visions reveal everything. All that is known will be unknown and what was lost will be found."*

"That prophecy is, like, mega." Corey Brandt whistled.

"We know." Celia groaned.

"I can't believe you read our prophecy on the Internet," said Oliver. "Isn't that, like, a violation of privacy?"

Qui shrugged.

"Do we really still have to do this whole

prophecy thing?" said Celia. "It seems kind of worn out."

"Honey." Her mother held her shoulders. "You have to fulfill a prophecy before it can be over."

"That is so totally unfair," said Celia.

"You say that a lot," said her father.

"Well." Celia shrugged. "Everybody needs a catchphrase."

Suddenly, sirens wailed on the street below.

"That will be the police," one of the warriors said. "We have to go. Follow us."

He turned and the warriors began moving across the roof.

"Wait!" Oliver rushed to catch up with the boy in the lead. "You didn't tell me your name!"

"I know I didn't." The boy smiled enigmatically, which Oliver would have known meant mysteriously if he had spent more time watching educational programming on TV instead of *Agent Zero* and *Bizarro Bandits*.

"Come on!" Oliver complained. "Why won't anyone explain anything? What's your name?"

"Sam," the boy answered.

"Sam?" said Oliver.

"What?" The boy wondered. "Sam is not a good name?"

"No," said Oliver. "It's fine. I was just expecting something more . . . I dunno. Exotic."

"Exotic?" Sam wondered.

"You know," Oliver said. "Like foreign."

"But you are the foreigners here," said Sam.

"Oh," said Oliver. "Right."

"Come this way."

"So where are we going?" Oliver jogged to keep up. "Sam! Hey, Sam! You can't just herd us like cows! Why are you being so mysterious? Why won't anyone ever explain anything?"

Oliver's complaints echoed across the rooftops of Djibouti, but no one answered his question. Sam now knew what Celia had discovered years ago: it was fun driving Oliver Navel crazy.

8

WE CATCH A FILM

BEHIND THEM, THEY heard the whine of fire engines racing to the burning hotel and the screech of police sirens racing after the pirates and the mob of goat herders.

The Dinka warriors, the tweens, their parents, Qui, their pets, Corey Brandt, his impersonator, and the professor climbed down from the rooftop to an empty square and crossed under a shady colonnade where a few women covered in brightly colored headscarves sold mangoes and vegetables and stinking piles of tiny fish. The women vanished into doorways as soon as they saw the Dinka warriors coming their way.

A few moments later, half a dozen armed pirates ran past the women in hot pursuit.

Just ahead of Oliver and Celia, a police jeep blocked their path.

"Stop!" two policemen in blue outfits called

out, pointing their rifles at the warriors, who froze. The pirates scattered and disappeared while the Navels put their hands into the air.

"You are under arrest by the authority of the Djibouti Police!" one of the police officers said and spoke quickly into his radio in Arabic.

"He said Djibouti." Oliver chuckled. Celia elbowed him.

"He's calling for backup," said Sam.

"I'm Corey Brandt!" Corey Brandt stepped forward, his hands high in the air, a friendly smile spread across his face. "From television's hit shows *Agent Zero, The Celebrity Adventurist*, and *Sunset High!*"

The police shouted and waved their guns at him. He stepped backward.

"I tried." He shrugged. "They're not fans."

Sensing the danger, or maybe just enjoying a good fight, Patrick and Beverly charged forward through Oliver's legs. The monkey jumped onto the head of one policeman while Beverly hissed and snapped her jaws at the other one. The police dropped their guns and dove into their jeep, locking their doors. Oliver smirked. He'd grown to like Beverly quite a lot.

Dennis clucked. Being a chicken, he was often

left out of the action, which was too bad. Chickens can be frightfully vicious when they want to be.

The warriors looked at the animals who had subdued the police, looked at each other, and shrugged. They picked up their spears again and kept running past the police jeep. The Navels and their entourage followed. As soon as they turned a corner, Bonnie and her pirates appeared ahead of them.

"Aha!" Bonnie shouted.

Dennis the chicken charged toward her, clucking wildly. The pirates were more confused than frightened, but it gave everyone a chance to turn back and run the other way again, past the jeep with the frightened police officers, through the square, and down another alley. Dennis raced after them to keep up, and the pirates, enraged at having let a chicken distract them, gave chase.

At that point, the women selling vegetables decided to pack up and call it a day.

"You can run but you can't hide!" Bonnie shouted after the Navels, although she kept one of her goons in front of her in case one of the warriors threw his spear. "I'm your worst nightmare," she taunted, unleashing a barrage of cheesy threats. Celia wondered if Bonnie knew she was acting like a second-rate TV villain. She really needed to get scarier lines.

As they turned down a side street, the mob of goat herders blocked their path.

"Raaarw!" the mob shouted, as mobs so often do. They charged forward.

Oliver and Celia ran around the corner to the left while everyone else ran to the right. The twins ducked through the alleys as fast as they could, turning and weaving, before they noticed they were suddenly alone. They were about to turn back when they heard the roar of the mob nearby. They kept running and found themselves in front of a wide blue door.

Celia pushed, but it didn't open.

"Let me do it," said Oliver, taking a step back and throwing himself at the door with his shoulder. He bounced off.

"Ow!" He slumped down, holding his shoulder. "That looks easier on TV."

"Oh. It's a pull door, not a push," said Celia and casually pulled the door open. She stepped over her brother. "Come on," she said. "We'll hide in here until the mob passes."

She gestured for Oliver to go first. He grunted

and scampered inside and Celia shut the door behind him.

They weren't exactly inside. The room was
large and had four thick stone walls but no ceiling. There were rows and rows of chairs spread
out in front of them and there was a hole cut out
of the wall above the chairs. Behind them was a
narrow stage with a big white screen along the
back. A big concrete tower rose from the side of
the building, with rusty old letters wrapped
around it.

"ODEON," Oliver read out loud. "I think this is
some kind of movie theater."

"You should be a superhero," said Celia. "Captain Obvious."

They heard police sirens wailing past them.

"I think if this were TV we wouldn't be super-
heroes," said Oliver. "We'd be the bad guys."

"Our parents just stole a truck from some goat
herders and burned down a hotel in the middle of
a city, and we used a poisonous lizard and a monkey to threaten the police just before sneaking
into a movie theater," said Celia. "I think even in
real life we're the bad guys now."

"This is so *Bizarro Bandits*," said Oliver. His
sister did not disagree with him.

"I can't believe we thought we could help Mom and Dad find Atlantis," Celia said. "We can't even get out of this city. We are just not supposed to be explorers."

"But what about the prophecy?" Oliver wondered.

"Maybe it was all a mistake. Like, it was given to the wrong kids."

"I don't think prophecies work like that."

"I'm going to check if the coast is clear," said Celia, cracking open the door they'd come through to peek out. Oliver looked around. There were mannequins all along the side wall, each dressed like a famous character from a classic movie. There were even a few from famous child actors back in the early black-and-white days of film. Oliver didn't recognize any of them. He looked up at the hole in the wall.

"That must be the projection booth," he said out loud, and glanced away to make sure his sister hadn't heard him. Maybe he really was Captain Obvious. When he looked back at the hole, a beam of light shot out toward the screen. He turned around. The picture was washed out in the sunlight, so it was hard to make out exactly what he was seeing. He figured that the movie theater must only get used at night. He squinted to study the picture.

He saw a bearded old man on a ship, battling a giant squid with a large spear. The man's hair hung down over one of his eyes and he was shouting to the sky, but the movie had no sound. Oliver didn't recognize the actor. It couldn't have been an American movie. He would have seen the ads for it before.

"That looks just like the kraken we fought in the Pacific Ocean," Oliver said, but Celia's head was poking out into the alleyway and she couldn't hear him.

The scene changed suddenly to a picture of the same man with the white beard fighting pirates.

"Must be a 'coming soon' kind of thing," Oliver said.

The scene changed again, now showing the man crossing mountains as shadowy snow creatures watched from caves, their eyes aglow.

"Those are just like the yetis we met in Tibet . . ." Oliver stepped closer to the screen, trying to make out what sort of movie this might be an ad for. His heart was pounding against his rib cage.

He saw the bearded man in a jungle somewhere, walking with a tribe of painted warriors toward a golden city, and the warriors looked a lot like they were from Qui's tribe.

"Bizarro," Oliver whispered, looking around once more for a hidden camera crew playing a practical joke.

Then the scene froze. It showed a snowy plain with a glowing city in the distance. The city had a large temple in the center surrounded by rings of walls stretching out across the snow. It looked just like the drawing of Atlantis in Percy Fawcett's journal. Suddenly, the bearded man appeared on the screen, leaning against a large tree and looking down at the city. A rainbow came down from the sky and the man walked right onto it, strolling toward the city. The scene didn't show his face, but he had a sack over his shoulder, and the sack was embroidered with the symbol of a key.

Oliver felt his stomach drop into his toes. The key was the symbol of the Mnemones, the guardians of the Lost Library of Alexandria. His mother's secret society.

"No way!" said Oliver.

"Come on!" Celia turned back around. "The coast is clear. Let's go find Mom and Da— What are you doing?"

Oliver stood in the center of the aisle, his head titled all the way back, looking up at the screen with his jaw hanging open. Celia worried that her brother had gone crazy. Maybe the strain of the day had been too much for him. Maybe he'd gotten toxic parasites. Celia shook her head. She hated how fragile little brothers' brains could be.

"It. Is. Time. To. Go," she said very slowly, so he could understand even if he had a toxic parasite in his brain.

Oliver pointed up.

"What?" said Celia. "It's just an ad for some foreign movie. It probably has subtitles. That's how movies trick you into reading."

Oliver grabbed the backpack and pulled out the old explorer's journal.

"Just look closely," he said as he flipped pages in the journal.

"It looks like some Christmas movie," said Celia. "Like Santa Claus has to save Christmas or somethi—oh." Celia's jaw dropped. She saw her mother's symbol and then the film looped back to the beginning again. She saw the scenes of the bearded man battling the kraken and meeting the tribe in the jungle and being watched by the yetis. "Oh no." Celia gulped.

Oliver held up the page in the journal he was looking for. It was what he'd seen back in the hotel room, the drawings of the bearded man. They looked just like the man in the movie. And the rest of the pictures were there too, on the screen and in the journal.

Celia looked at the page and started shaking her head slowly back and forth.

"No way," she said. "It can't be."

"I think so," said Oliver.

He flipped through the pages and showed the giant tree drawings that filled the last pages of the journal. It was the same tree in the movie.

"That's why the catalog showed us that book by the saint."

"Saint Nicholas," said Oliver. "I think we have to tell Mom and Dad."

"Tell them what?" his sister said, although she knew. It just sounded too crazy to actually say out loud.

"We have to tell them that we need to go to the North Pole," Oliver said. "If we want to find Atlantis, we have to find Santa Claus."

It didn't sound any less crazy when her brother said it out loud.

9

WE'RE NOT PROJECTING

"OLIVER! CELIA!" THEY heard their parents voices on the street, whisper-shouting their names.

"Let's go," sighed Celia, opening the door and gesturing for her brother to go first. "You do the talking," she added.

"Me?" Oliver stopped in the hallway. "Why me?"

"Because you saw the movie first!"

"But—" Oliver really didn't want to have to explain this to his parents. If they were wrong, they would sound like lunatics, like they'd gone just as crazy as the contestants at the end of *Bizarro Bandits.* If they were right, they would be dragged off to the snowy reaches of the North Pole.

Neither option was appealing.

"If you hadn't turned on *Celebrity Fashion Crimes* I never would have seen all those drawings in the journal."

"Well, that just shows you that you should pay more attention to fashion."

Oliver knew he'd never win the argument with his sister.

"Over here!" Celia whisper-shouted back into the street.

"Oh, thank goodness!" Their mother rushed inside the movie theater, hugging the children tightly. "We thought you'd been captured."

"No," said Oliver. "We actually found—"

"Why did you wander off?" Sam asked Oliver, as the rest of the rescue party streamed inside. "It is not safe."

"I know that," Oliver said. "But we found this thing and we—"

"Come on," said Dr. Navel. "Corey's already arranged for a private jet to get us out of here!"

"This is a pretty cool old movie theater," said Corey. "I wonder if they'd want to do a Corey Brandt film festival."

"You'd want to come back to Djibouti?" Celia was shocked.

Corey giggled at the word Djibouti. Celia rolled her eyes.

"We should go before the police or the pirates

or the goat herders find us here," said Dr. Navel.

"Yeah, but we saw this thing and it means we—" Oliver was still trying to tell everyone what they'd seen.

"Come on," said Qui, peeking out at the street again. "The coast is clear."

"We have to find Santa Claus!" Oliver declared.

Everyone turned to stare at him. The hot sun over Djibouti blazed down. Sam closed the door again. A bead of sweat drizzled down Oliver's forehead. "I mean, er, to find Atlantis . . . um, see, uh . . . there's a movie." He pointed at the screen behind him but it was blank. No light shined from the projection booth. "Well, there was a movie," said Oliver.

Dr. Navel squinted at Oliver and Celia with a look that said "I wonder if both of my children have toxic parasites?"

"There really was a movie!" Celia said. "We're not crazy."

"Of course you're not crazy, honey." Their mother nodded. "But if you saw a movie here, someone must have been showing it, right? Which means we're not alone here."

All eyes turned to the dark projection booth above the seats. All ears listened carefully for any sounds of movement. Oliver and Celia felt knots tying in their stomachs. Had someone been watching them the whole time?

Their mother ran to the back of the theater and climbed onto the chairs, hoisting herself into the dark booth.

"Be careful!" Dr. Navel warned, long after it would have been helpful advice.

The twins watched the opening in the wall, too nervous to breathe.

"It's okay!" their mother called. "There's no one here." She climbed out and trotted back down the aisle to her family.

"If there is no one there," wondered Professor Rasmali-Greenberg, "then who showed the children a film?"

"No one," said their mother. "There's no film in the projector."

"Maybe they ran away?" suggested Celia.

"There's no bulb in the projector either," said their mother. "Nor is there electricity running to it. It could not have been turned on."

"C-r-e-e-p-y," Corey spelled.

"So . . . um." Qui scratched the back of her neck. "Who is Santa Claus?"

"You don't know who Santa is?" Oliver asked. "Old Saint Nick? Like, uh, Father Christmas?"

"Is Santa Claus an ancestor of yours?" Qui wondered. "Do you pray to him?"

Oliver looked to Celia. She crossed her arms. She wasn't going to explain it.

"Uh, I guess, sort of." Oliver shrugged. He didn't really want to explain about Christmas and stockings and presents and Santa's lists of who'd been naughty and who'd been nice. Somehow, it felt really embarrassing to talk about, even though he knew that everyone had their beliefs and his were no better or worse than anyone else's. They all sounded strange to outsiders.

"There are more things in heaven and earth, Horatio, Than are dreamt of in your philosophy," said their mother. The kids looked at her with puzzled expressions.

"William Shakespeare?" she said. *"Hamlet?* What do you all learn in school these days?"

"We're in sixth grade, Mom," said Celia. "We don't read *Hamlet*."

"The point is," their mother said, "the world

has no end of wonders. Think of everything you've seen and done. You've climbed mountains in Tibet. You've explored jungles and oceans, met witches and monsters and villains."

"And a talking yak," said Oliver.

"And a talking yak," agreed his mother. "So you see . . . why shouldn't Santa Claus lead the way to Atlantis?"

"Because he's not real," said Celia.

"How do you know?" Oliver objected.

"I just do."

"Do not."

"Do too."

"Do not."

"We must go." One of the warriors came over to the interrupt them.

"Agreed." Dr. Navel peered outside again. "Everyone on the streets is looking for us, though. How will we make it to the airfield?"

"I have an idea." Sam smiled and spoke to his elders in their language. He pointed to the mannequins along the wall. The elders had a brief discussion and then Sam turned to Ernest, the celebrity impersonator. He borrowed a pen from Dr. Navel and approached Ernest, holding the pen like a spear.

"One more show," said Sam, as Ernest groaned his objections through the gag in his mouth, backing away from the young Dinka warrior, his eyes wide with fear.

10
WE GO AHEAD

"YOU AREN'T LYING to me, are you?" Bonnie demanded.

The market woman shook her head inside her colorful scarf. Bonnie's knife tapped against the fabric while the other pirates held the woman's arms behind her back.

"Why would they go into a movie theater?" Bonnie asked.

The woman started speaking frantically, but Bonnie didn't understand a word of her language. She spat on the ground at the woman's feet. "It was a rhetorical question," she said. She nodded at her men and they let the woman go. Bonnie grabbed a mango from one of the woman's baskets and took a bite out of it, skin and all.

"Bleck." She spat. "This isn't even ripe." She tossed the mango to the ground in front of the woman, walking away without paying for it. Pirates, as we all know, do not like to pay for anything they can simply steal.

As they walked away the woman muttered oaths under her breath and pulled her cell phone from her robe. She sent a quick text message and looked to the alley by her market stall, where a Dinka warrior received the message. He looked up from his phone and nodded a thank-you to the woman. Then he waved behind him.

The market woman watched as an odd assemblage of foreigners followed the warrior from the alley. Among them were a lizard, a monkey, a chicken, two adults, and two children, all dressed like characters from classic movies; a girl wearing a colorful wool hat despite the desert heat and a teenager who looked a lot like the famous Corey Brandt.

Bonnie and her goons approached the Odeon Cinema. It was easy enough to find, with its large rusted sign. It was the only movie theater in Djibouti. It did seem fitting that the couch potatoes and the celebrity would hide out there. Bonnie studied the posters by the front door advertising that evening's showing. Some mindless action movie. Bonnie did not like action movies. She found the life of a pirate active enough. She enjoyed romantic comedies, although she could never admit that in front of her pirate crew. They'd laugh at her and then they'd try to do to her what she'd done to the previous captain. She did not care to become shark bait just because she enjoyed a big-screen kiss from time to time.

"All right, boys," she said. "The Navels have escaped too many times. I don't want to take any chances this time. Don't ask questions and don't talk to them. No clever lines. This isn't some movie and we aren't some movie villains. The only one of them who's worth anything is Corey Brandt. Capture him. The rest you can gut like fish for all I care. We leave no other survivors."

"What about the warriors?" asked one of the pirates, who did not care to go into hand-to-hand combat with a seven-foot-tall champion of desert warfare. He'd gone into piracy because he liked the loot, not because he liked taking a spear to the head.

"And what about the lizard?" asked another, who had seen what Beverly had done to his shipmates.

Bonnie didn't answer. She steadied the grip on her knife and charged the front entrance to the cinema. With a few quick kicks, the doors burst open against their hinges and the pirates streamed through the small lobby and into the open-air auditorium.

"You know that was a pull door?" one of the pirates called as they ran through. "We didn't need to break it."

"Aha!" Bonnie shouted, ignoring the man. The Navels were sitting low in their seats, watching the blank screen. She recognized the backs of two small heads and she saw Corey Brandt next to them, looking around nervously.

Had she been a more thoughtful woman, Bonnie might have wondered why the famous teenager was wearing a gag, but she was not a thoughtful woman. She was filled with bloodlust and she charged, tackling the teenager to the ground, while her men used their heavy knives to take off the Navels' heads with powerful swipe.

The twins' small heads hit the ground with hollow thumps. Their white-plastic bodies slumped forward onto the dusty floor.

"Mannequins!" Bonnie cried.

The wigs rolled into the dirt.

Bonnie looked down at Corey. Her eyes narrowed. She wiped her thumb under his eye, and once again his teardrop freckle rubbed away.

"Ernest!" she groaned. "We've been tricked!"

"It's worse than that," said one of her men. "We're trapped!"

Dinka warriors, more than Bonnie could count, appeared atop the wall all around them. Their faces popped up from the projection booth. They rushed in from the side doors and the front doors, their spears poised. The pirates were surrounded. They dropped their weapons and put their hands up.

Well, all but one of them.

"Cowards!" yelled Bonnie. "I am your captain! Fight with me!"

"Pass," said one the pirates.

"No thanks," said another.

A third answered in Dutch and a fourth in Chinese, but their meaning was clear enough.

"Well, you'll never take me alive!" Bonnie yelled at the warriors.

Sam, standing beside his elders on the high wall, shrugged.

"If that's what you want!" he called down.

The other pirates took a few steps away from Bonnie.

"We're fine with being taken alive!" one of them called. "We surrender! Take us! Take us alive!"

Bonnie crouched in an attack position.

"Mrrrm!" Ernest groaned as she stepped on his hand, stumbling backward and hitting her head on the ground.

When she woke, she and her men were tied around the old rusty Odeon sign for all the city to see, as the Djibouti police argued about how best to get the pirates down and take them to prison. Ernest was tied up with them, but his gag had finally slipped from his mouth.

"I'm not with them!" he shouted. "I'm innocent! I'm Corey Brandt!"

"Where's your freckle?" one of the police officers demanded and Ernest had no answer to that. He sighed as he saw a small plane take off in the distance, lifting over the city and taking a hard turn over the ocean.

"I thought so," the officer called. "You are all under arrest for piracy, destruction of property, and disturbing the peace of Djibouti!"

In spite of everything, Ernest cracked a smile.

Djibouti.

It really was a funny name for a city.

11

WE ARE AND ARE NOT

"SO TELL ME about Santa Claus," their mother said over the roar of the jet engines as they flew away from Djibouti aboard a private plane Corey had chartered in the desert. Being rich and famous had its advantages.

Oliver looked over at his sister. She looked back at him. Neither of them wanted to go first, because they were starting to wonder if they'd imagined the whole thing. It was too crazy to be real, right?

"Well," Oliver started. "I was looking through the old explorer's journal we found in the Amazon and I saw these drawings of, like, Atlantis and stuff. And there was this guy in all of them who looked a lot like . . . you know . . ."

"Santa Claus?" said Corey Brandt.

"Yeah. And then we were in that movie theater, hiding from the pirates, and I, like, saw these visions of, you know . . ."

"Santa Claus?" said Corey Brandt.

Oliver nodded. "Celia saw them too. She also thought the guy looked like . . . you know . . ."

"Santa Cl—" Corey started.

"I did not," said Celia. "It was just some bearded guy doing explorery things. It wasn't, like, a guy in a red suit with presents and stuff. I mean, he had a sack and white hair, but he could have been anyone." She didn't want Corey to think she was totally nuts.

"That's totally nuts," said Corey.

Celia sighed.

"Yeah, I guess it is kind of stupid." She blushed. "But he did look a lot like—"

"No, no," Corey interrupted her. "It's totally nuts because I was just thinking about making a TV Christmas special called *Saint Nick of Time*, where Santa Claus fights a zombie invasion of the North Pole to save the holiday season."

"Okay," said Oliver. "Now that is nuts."

"I think it's based on a book," said Corey.

"You know," Qui said, leaning on the back of Celia's seat, "maybe the man you saw is

Santa Claus and also not Santa Claus."

"Don't you start getting all mysterious too," Oliver grumbled.

"I think Qui understands this perfectly," said Claire Navel. "In America we call Saint Nicholas by the name Santa Claus. He is based on the fourth-century Greek Saint Nicholas from the island of Myra, a worker of miracles and giver of gifts. In the Dutch tradition, he's called Sinter-klaas, and in some legends, he's also been known as the Lord of the Sea."

"Like Poseidon," said Oliver. "The ancient Greek god of the sea."

"And the patron of Atlantis," added Celia.

"Okay," their father called back to them. "How did you guys know that?"

"Educational programming," the twins answered together.

"You know there are also those who believe in the Norse tradition," said Professor Rasmali-Greenberg, turning around in his seat. "You see, some believe that Santa Claus is related to the ancient Norse god Odin, the All-Father, who lived in the great city of Asgard, who drank from the well of wisdom, and who watched the universe from the Tree of the World."

"There were a lot of trees in the explorer's journal," said Oliver.

"You all realize how crazy this is, right?" said Celia, who did not think anyone was reacting to this theory the way they should have. "I mean, Santa Claus and Poseidon?"

"And Odin, the All-Father," added Oliver.

"Right," said Celia. "It can't possibly have anything to do with Atlantis. There's not even such a thing as Santa Claus!"

"Is too," said Oliver.

"Is not!" said Celia.

"Is too," said Oliver.

"It's not crazy at all," their mother said, stopping their argument. "In 1679, Count Olof Rudbeck in Sweden proposed the same theory about Atlantis in the Arctic as the home of all the ancient Norse gods and monsters. Asgard, city of the gods, could be Atlantis. Odin could be Santa Claus. Count Olof never made that connection, but you just did. You might have completed the chain of knowledge started long, long ago. Isn't that exciting?"

"No," the twins said in unison.

"People have said Atlantis was in a lot of places throughout history," the professor told them. "Everywhere from the Amazonian rainforest to the coast of Spain, and yet it has never yet been found."

"Because nobody looked to the north." Dr. Navel smiled. "Everyone was looking for Poseidon's great civilization under the water, but no one looked under ice. No one was looking for Santa Claus."

"You know the old saying about finding things?" their mother asked. "How they're always in the last place you look? Well, we've looked everywhere else for Atlantis, so why not the North Pole?"

"Lost things are always in the last place you look," said Celia, "because you wouldn't keep looking for them after you found them." Celia glanced at Oliver. He nodded. "And that's why, we think, like, just this once, we want to go with you."

"What?" said their father.

"What?" said their mother.

"Bwak," said Dennis the chicken.

"Well, like everyone's always telling us"— Oliver nodded at Qui—"there's a prophecy. Visions and greatest explorers and all that."

"And we figured you'd never find Atlantis without us," added Celia. "And this way, we can be done. This can be the last place we look."

Their parents looked at each other, amazed. Never in their wildest dreams did they imagine Oliver and Celia actually wanting to go exploring with them.

"Don't get the wrong idea," said Celia. "This isn't going to be a regular thing. It's just this once."

"So that we can all stay together, like a normal family," said Oliver.

"Even though normal families never have to escape from mobs of goat herders and bloodthirsty pirates in Djibouti," said Celia. She scowled at Oliver before he could laugh.

"Djibouti." The professor chuckled under his breath.

Celia sighed. "And when this is over, we want our own TVs in each of our rooms," she said.

"Big ones," added Oliver.

"With flat screens."

Their parents grinned at each other from ear to ear. Their mother reached over and hit a button on the intercom to the pilot.

"Captain," she said. "Take us north. We're going to the Svalbard archipelago."

"That's near the North Pole?" asked Celia.

Her mother nodded.

"Did you know that in the North Pole, every direction is south?" their father asked. "Isn't that amazing! When you're at the North Pole, everywhere is below you!"

"Great." Celia groaned. "Nowhere to go but down."

Dr. Navel ignored her. He patted her on the head and went with their mother to look over maps.

"How will we find this Atlantis place when we get there?" Qui squished into the seat next to Celia.

"Our parents will figure that out." Oliver shrugged.

"They've never figured any of this stuff out before." Celia shook her head. "Why would they start now?"

"So what do you think we should do, if you're such a great explorer?" Oliver asked.

"I didn't say I'm a great explorer," said Celia. "I just said that we'll probably figure this out before Mom and Dad do, because that's, like, what always happens."

"Maybe something different will happen this time," Oliver said. "Maybe they'll save the day and we can just relax."

"Mom said *we* have to finish this prophecy before we can go home," said Celia. "Not her. Us."

"Can I help?" asked Corey.

"Yeah, could you explain the prophecy to us and tell us what to do?" said Oliver. Corey scratched his head but didn't answer. Oliver looked at Qui.

"How would I know?" she said.

"You were in our visions in the Amazon," said Celia. "You helped guide us."

"Those were your visions," Qui said, shaking her head. "I'm not psychic or magic or anything," she explained. "It's like on your TV. I was just the antenna on the television set, not the show. I helped you pick up the broadcast signal. I'm just a kid like you."

"Not really like us," said Oliver.

"I know that that one line from the prophecy, *the greatest explorers shall be the least*, is about us," said Celia. "We're the least."

"The least what?" asked Oliver.

"The least whatever. The least old. The least interested. The least adventurous."

Qui and Corey nodded. No one would disagree with that.

"That also means that we're the greatest," said Oliver.

"So Santa is and is not Santa, and you are and are not the greatest," Corey repeated.

"I guess so," said Celia.

There was a long silence as they considered that possibility. They listened to the loud drone of the airplane engines with wrinkled brows and pursed lips.

Oliver finally broke the quiet with an idea that had just occurred to him.

"Hey, maybe when we're in the Arctic we'll get to ride dogsleds." Oliver smiled.

Riding on dogsleds across the Svalbard archipelago sounded just like something *Agent Zero* would do. He looked over at Corey, who looked pretty excited too. They high-fived each other. Celia grunted and the boys stopped smiling.

Celia had agreed to go on this adventure, but she had never agreed to enjoy it.

12

WE TURN THE PAGE

"**DON'T TELL ME** you don't understand. I know you understand because this is perfectly understandable to someone of your understanding!" Sir Edmund slammed his fist down on the long wooden table.

"Uh . . . what?" quivered the explorer at the opposite end of the table, squinting in the bright light that shone into his eyes and not understanding anything the little man had just shouted at him.

The explorer was not tied up or held at the point of a spear or a gun or a weapon of any sort, and yet it should be quite clear to us, by his darting eyes and the nervous tapping of his fingers on the table and the pools of sweat soaking through his shirt jacket, that he was indeed a prisoner. On either side of the table, stern men in dark suits watched the explorer carefully.

"I don't understand what you're asking me," he squeaked.

"Poppycock!" Sir Edmund slammed his fist on the table again. "Balderdash! Flimflammery!"

"I don't understand that either," the explorer cried.

"Edmund," said the only man at the table who was not wearing a suit. He wore a T-shirt and blue jeans and had a baseball cap pulled low over his face. He hardly looked up from his cell phone, on which he was tapping away sending text messages. "Your question was confusing."

"It's *Sir* Edmund," Sir Edmund said.

The man stopped tapping on his phone. He, like everyone at the table but the explorer, wore a gold ring engraved with a symbol of a scroll locked in chains, the symbol of the Council, enemies of the Mnemones from time immemorial. He fiddled with the ring but didn't say a word.

The other figures on the Council held their breath, waiting. Sir Edmund's nostrils flared.

"Did I forget to call you sir?" The man in the baseball cap smiled. "Oops." He shrugged and went back to sending text messages.

"Ahem." Sir Edmund cleared his throat loudly. "Ahem," he tried again. No one else spoke. The captive explorer shifted uncomfortably in his chair. All eyes looked toward the man in the baseball cap, who finally looked up from his phone.

"What? Are we done already?" he asked.

"I would appreciate it if you would give these proceedings your full attention," Sir Edmund told him.

"This is the tenth explorer we've questioned," the man answered. "None of them know how to read that map of yours, and we're just wasting time. We should be going after the Navels. Unless you're afraid that they'll beat you again."

"They have never beaten me at anything!" Sir Edmund's face was bright red.

"So your ship sank itself in the Pacific Ocean? The Navels didn't do that?"

"A treacherous giant squid sank my ship," Sir Edmund answered. "Anyway, I got Plato's map to Atlantis, so I won. The Navels lost."

"What about getting you kicked out of the Explorers Club?" the man smirked.

"I was not kicked out!" Sir Edmund objected. "I left on purpose. I wanted to start my own club!"

"Oh yes." The man laughed. "The Gentleman's Adventuring Society . . . an appropriate acronym."

"What do you mean by that?"

"An acronym is a word formed from the first letters of other words," the man answered.

"I know what an acronym is, you dolt!" Sir Edmund yelled at him. "But what do you mean by insulting the Gentleman's Adventuring Society!"

"I have nothing against GAS," the man answered. "I get it all the time."

The others around the table chuckled behind their hands. Sir Edmund clenched his fists and seethed at them in silence until they were finished. He was their leader, but he knew they were losing patience with him. His power was brought into question at every turn, and if he did not produce results soon he might lose control of the Council for good.

"You!" He pointed down the table at the frightened explorer. "I demand that you answer me now."

"But I don't remember the question," the explorer said.

Sir Edmund's eyes nearly popped out of his head in anger.

"My question is this," he said, trying to keep from shouting again. "Where, in your expert opinion as a scholar of the lost civilization of Atlantis, do you suspect is its true and final location, based on the evidence presented on this map we have placed in front of you?"

The scholar looked nervously at the old map in front of him, with its strangely shaped continents and mysterious ancient Greek writing.

"Well . . . you see . . . I . . . ," he stammered.

"Enough of this, Edmund." The man in the baseball cap stood. "He clearly can't read the map! We'll never find Atlantis this way. This so-called scholar is just as useless as all the others."

"I am not useless!" the scholar objected. "I am an expert on Ice Age archaeology."

"Whatever that means," grumbled the man in the baseball cap.

The scholar's face flushed with anger. "It means I have dug up the bones of the saber-toothed tiger and the ancient pliosaur! I have discovered the rune stones of Viking kings and I have had papers published in *Weird Science Magazine*!"

"I'm sure your parents are very proud of you," Sir Edmund said, cutting him off.

"I demand to be returned to my research station in Svalbard!"

"Of course," said Sir Edmund. "Just tell us how to read Plato's map."

"You know," the man with the baseball hat said, "*The Daytime Doctor* describes insanity as repeating the same action over and over and expecting a different result."

"Don't tell me about *The Daytime Doctor*. Television is for lazy minds," grumbled Sir Edmund.

"Well." The man stood. "I am not waiting around here any longer. I have important business to attend to."

"We'll text you if anything important happens," Sir Edmund sneered sarcastically.

"See that you do." The man in the baseball cap turned to leave. He stopped in front of the door and turned back to Sir Edmund. "By the way, I heard that the Navels just staged a daring rescue in Djibouti and escaped on a private plane with Corey Brandt. Looks like they've gotten ahead of you . . . again." He smirked and left the room, slamming the door behind him.

Sir Edmund looked back to the explorer. "Tell me what Plato's map says."

"How could I possibly read this map?" the explorer whined. "I know nothing about Plato!"

"He was an ancient Greek philosopher," said Sir Edmund. "He wrote the earliest descriptions we have of the lost city of Atlantis. Surely you must know something about him!"

"No." The scholar crossed his arms. "Nothing."

"So you cannot read this map?" One of the well-dressed men leaned forward.

"No one can!" the scholar cried. "There is no key on it! Without a key, we don't know which way is north, or how far these places are supposed to be from each other, or what is a city and what is a mountain. The only thing I recognize is the picture of a dragon on the side."

"So there are dragons?" Sir Edmund leaned forward.

"No," said the scholar. "Dragons were often used to decorate maps. They don't mean anything. Or maybe they do. Without a key, the whole map is just a pretty drawing. And anyway, like I said, I don't know anything about Plato's map!"

"You're lying," said Sir Edmund.

"I am not," said the scholar.

"You are," said Sir Edmund.

"I am not," said the scholar.

They went on like that for several minutes as the rest of the Council snapped their heads back and forth between one end of the table and the other.

"Enough." Sir Edmund threw his hands in the air in disgust and dropped down onto his chair. All the men of the Council turned to look at him. Because he was a very small man, only the top of his head down to his large red mustache could be seen.

"May I go back to my research station?" the explorer asked. "If I don't return soon, I will be missed. Someone will come looking for me."

"No." Sir Edmund didn't even look at the scholar. "You live alone at a research station in the Arctic Circle. No one will even notice you're gone."

He reached underneath the table and pulled out a small stone tablet with squiggles and lines carved into it. When the scholar saw it, his eyes went wide.

"That's . . . that's the rune stone of Nidhogg!" the scholar cried. "How did you get that?"

"I purchased it from a collector," said Sir Edmund. "You'd be amazed what you can get when you have millions of dollars to spend." He nodded to one of his men guarding the door, who came over to the table with a sledgehammer and lifted it high. "Tell me what I want to know, or the stone will be destroyed."

"You wouldn't!" cried the scholar. "That is a priceless artifact. One of a kind. It tells the myth of Nidhogg the dragon, trapped at the root of the world tree, dreaming of release and revenge."

"Yes," said Sir Edmund. "I believe it is also the greatest discovery you have ever made?"

The scholar nodded.

"It'd be shame to see it destroyed," said Sir Edmund.

The scholar gulped but didn't answer.

Sir Edmund signaled the man with the sledgehammer, who tightened his grip and prepared to pulverize the ancient artifact.

"Wait! Stop!" cried the scholar. "Lord, forgive me. I will tell you what you want to know."

The scholar took his fingers and turned the map slowly so that the top and bottom became the sides.

Sir Edmund smiled widely. What had looked like a rough coastline became a canyon at the top of the world, a dragon perched neatly inside it, looking down at the world below; what had seemed to be a mysterious landmass took on the rough shape of a very recognizable continent, land and sea and mountain looked strikingly familiar.

"Oh Plato, you clever devil." Sir Edmund smiled, studying the map. "It's always in the last place you look." He laughed to himself.

The rest of the Council leaned forward, expectant.

"Gentlemen," he exhaled. "In his ancient manuscript, Plato described Atlantis as lying 'beyond the Pillars of Hercules.' In his time, that was the end of the known world. Everyone believed he meant the passage from the Mediterranean Sea into the Atlantic Ocean, but if there were more than one set of these pillars, a set in the far north, for example, then he could have been describing a great city in the north, which would now covered by the frozen ice of the Arctic Ocean."

"Just to be perfectly clear," one of the men said. "You are saying that Atlantis is somewhere in the Arctic Ocean?"

"I am saying," Sir Edmund stood and raised his arm like he was posing for a portrait, "that it is at the very top, that frozen land where the Viking warriors had placed their gods, where children dream of Santa Claus, and where I—"

"Ahem," another Council member interrupted Sir Edmund's speech with an exaggerated cough.

"Yes, yes," grumbled Sir Edmund. "Where *we* will reach our destiny! The North Pole."

"And what of the Navels?" a man asked. "We cannot have them get in our way again."

Sir Edmund rolled his eyes. "Don't worry about the Navels. I have a plan for them." He drew a finger across his throat in a gesture whose meaning was perfectly clear.

13

WE HAVE A CATCH PHRASE

"I, LIKE, REALLY wanted to thank you guys for coming back to rescue me," Corey told the twins. Their parents were chatting with the professor about sea ice and walrus migration at the front of the airplane.

"I know you guys hate adventures," Corey added.

"We don't hate adventures," Celia said. "We just like not-adventures more."

"Well, I promise when we I get back to Hollywood, I'm going to do something awesome to say thank you."

"Like what?" Oliver wondered. Sometimes, what other people thought was awesome, Oliver and Celia thought was boring, dangerous, or both at the same time.

"How would you two like to see your story

turned into a TV movie-of-the-week?" Corey smirked.

"Network or cable?" Celia raised her eyebrows.

"Network," Corey said.

Celia frowned.

"Or cable!" Corey corrected. "Whatever you guys say!"

"Cool," the twins answered him.

"Could I be in the movie?" Oliver asked.

"They'll hire actors." Celia rolled her eyes.

"Will you play me, Corey?" Oliver smiled.

"Corey will play himself, dummy." His sister shook her head.

"Well, I want *someone* cool to play me," he told Corey.

"Someone cool?" Celia laughed. "It's not *Bizarro Bandits*!"

"Well, they'll have to find your actress on the Nature Network," Oliver snapped back at her. "Maybe there's a walrus that can act like a know-it-all."

"Maybe Corey'll just get Beverly to play you," said Celia. "The lizard's a lot smarter."

"I am smarter than a lizard!" Oliver objected.

"Guys." Corey held his hands up in surrender.

"Don't fight. I promise, you'll both be happy with the movie."

"Can we get that in writing?" Celia raised her eyebrows at the teenager.

"Celia thinks she's knows everything about the movie business because she watches *Access Celebrity Tonight*," said Oliver.

"Corey, can you put a scene in the movie where my brother loses the ability to speak so we finally get some peace and quiet?" Celia asked.

"But that never happened!" said Oliver.

"It's a movie," said Celia. "Corey can make stuff up that didn't happen to tell a better story."

"It wouldn't be a better story if I couldn't talk," said Oliver.

"It would for me," said Celia.

"Hey Corey," Oliver said. "Can you make up a scene where Celia jumps out of a plane and has to walk to the North Pole?"

"If anyone is jumping out of the plane," said Celia, "it's you."

"Is not," said Oliver.

"Is too," said Celia.

"Is not," said Oliver.

"Guys! Come on! Don't fight," Corey said.

"Is too," Celia added quietly, because she liked to have the last word.

"It seems like you guys argue all the time," said Corey. "I was never lucky enough to have a twin brother or sister. But if I were, I'd want him or her to be my best friend, not argue all the time."

"But," Oliver scratched his head, "me and Celia are best friends."

"Celia and I," Celia corrected him. "And yeah," she said to Corey. "We are."

"But you guys are always arguing!" Corey said.

"*The Daytime Doctor* says that arguments between siblings help young people develop important social skills, like logical thinking, emotional control, and verbal acuity," Celia explained.

"She means, like, being clever and talking fast," Oliver said.

"Talking well," corrected Celia. "Not just fast. I learned it from *Wally Worm's Word World: If you have acuity, you'll speak with ingenuity*," she said. "Ingenuity is like cleverness," she added, to make sure they understood.

"Know-it-all," Oliver muttered.

"So, uh." Corey's forehead wrinkled with

thought. "You guys, like, like to argue? And it's, like, good for you?"

"Yeah," said Oliver. "I didn't really mean that I'd be happier if Celia jumped out of the plane."

"And I didn't mean it either," said Celia. "I don't want Oliver jumping out of the plane. I don't want anyone jumping out of the plane."

"Bad news, guys!" Their father walked down the aisle toward them. "We can't land in Svalbard because there's too much ice on the runway . . . so we're going to have to jump out of the plane!"

Celia turned to her brother. "You totally jinxed us," she said.

"What? How did I do that?" Oliver replied.

"You brought up jumping out of a plane!" said Celia. "On TV, you can't talk about jumping out of a plane while you're on a plane. Because then you'll have to jump out of it!"

"That's not a rule," said Oliver.

"It is," said Celia.

"No," said Oliver. "You can't talk about *not wanting* to jump out of a plane. That's the rule! And you said, 'I don't want Oliver jumping out of the plane. I don't want anyone jumping out of the plane.' So this is your fault."

"That's not the rule," said Celia.

"Yes it is," said Oliver. "I know the rules: If you knock on a door and there's no answer, but it opens slowly anyway, something terrible will be on the other side. If you step onto ice that looks solid, it will crack. And if you talk about how you don't want to jump out of a plane, then you're going to have to jump out a plane, like, right then . . . it's fate."

"No," said Celia. "That's not fate. It's called dramatic irony."

"It's fate."

"It's dramatic irony."

"Fate."

"Irony!"

"Fate!"

"Irony!"

"Guys!" their father interrupted. "This isn't fate or irony. It's just what's happening."

"On TV, everything happens for a reason," said Oliver.

"But this isn't TV," said his father.

"The rules are the same," he said. "The TV people wouldn't make them up out of nowhere."

"If you say so," Dr. Navel said. "When I was your age, we had these crazy things called books."

"When you were our age, did your parents make you jump out of an airplane?" Oliver asked.

"Well no," said Dr. Navel. "I guess times change."

"I guess so." Celia scowled.

"There's more," Dr. Navel said. "We only have these two parachutes." He held up two big backpacks with all kinds of straps and buckles on them. "But we have the supplies for four of us to go with a tandem jump."

"Tandem?" Oliver looked at Celia, although he really wasn't sure he wanted to know the meaning of the word.

"Having two things close together," said Celia. *"Don't board the ark at random, come two by two, in tandem."*

"You guys really like *Wally Worm's Word World*," said Corey.

Celia nodded. Oliver shrugged.

"With only two parachutes, your mother and I can skydive with one of you attached to each of us."

"Which means that Corey can't come," said Oliver.

"Or Qui?" said Celia, glancing back at her friend.

Dr. Navel nodded. "Or the professor. Or the animals."

Patrick the monkey swished his tail, Dennis flapped his little chicken wings, and Beverly flicked her tongue, although what that meant was anyone's guess.

"But—" Oliver objected. He didn't have much more of an answer than that.

"That's not fair!" Celia said.

"I know it's not fair," said their mother, coming to the back of the plane. "It's not fair, but that's the way it is. Sometimes bad things happen to good people and good things happen to bad people, and sometimes good kids get chased out of Djibouti by pirates and have to jump out of airplanes without their friends so they can find lost cities in the Arctic Circle. Life is just like that."

"I don't think life is supposed to be like that," said Oliver.

"It is if you're a Navel," said Celia.

"It's okay, Oliver," Corey told him. "You have to fulfill your destiny now, right? The prophecy needs to be completed. That's, like, a rule too."

"I hate destiny," said Oliver.

Corey smiled sadly, and nodded. "But dude, it's just like commercials. Unavoidable."

"But we came to Djibouti to rescue you," Celia said, turning to Corey.

"It's, like, okay." He put his hands on her shoulders. "The professor and I will take your friends home and look after your pets. I need to go back to Hollywood anyway. I've got a movie to make about my coolest friends in the world."

"He means us," whispered Oliver.

"I know, doofus," she sniffled.

"So you go with your parents and save the day," said Corey. "It'll make an awesome ending to my movie."

"Okay," said Celia.

"Okay," said Oliver.

"We'll do it for the movie," added Celia. "It needs a good ending."

"All right, kids." Their mother clapped her hands together. "We are nearly over the Arctic Circle, so we have to get ready to jump. The plane will lower us to twenty thousand feet."

"I promise you," their father said, "skydiving is a lot of fun when you're doing it on purpose."

The twins glared at their mother, who had arranged for their last skydiving adventure over Tibet, which had not been on purpose at all.

"Let's just get this over with," said Celia.

"You say that a lot," her father told her.

"Yeah, well, everyone needs a catchphrase." She frowned, realizing that she actually now had two.

Their parents clipped all the straps and clasps so they were each tied together, Oliver to his mom and Celia to her dad.

"Bye, Beverly," Oliver told the lizard. She flicked her tongue, which was as close to a good-bye as a *Heloderma horridum* could give. "Don't bite anyone while I'm gone," he added. "Unless you have to."

"Ride a dogsled for me," said Corey. "Just like *Agent Zero* would." He gave Oliver another high-five.

"See you soon, Celia," said Qui, groggy from her nap. Her eyes were puffy from sleeping.

"See you," said Celia and they hugged. They didn't say good-bye, we should note, because that is the hardest thing to say to a friend and is best avoided, especially when one friend is about to jump out of an airplane on a dangerous adventure. When they separated, Qui's eyes were still puffy, but not from sleeping.

Claire Navel stepped to the door of the plane

with Oliver strapped the front of her like he was a baby kangaroo in a pouch.

"Don't look down!" she shouted into his ear as she put her feet to the edge. Oliver was now hanging completely outside the airplane. He felt himself being pulled by the wind. He looked down. He kind of had to. That was also, like, a rule.

The island of Svalbard was just a white speck in the ice-blue ocean far below. In the distance he could actually see the curve of the Earth and the dark nothing beyond.

Oliver bent his neck around to the side to shout back into the plane at his sister, who was strapped to their father. "Why do I always have to go first?" he yelled.

"Everyone needs a catchphrase," Celia shouted back at him.

Oliver frowned as his mother leaped into the sky.

14

WE FEEL LIKE FALCONS

"AAH!" OLIVER YELLED, and also, "WAH!" And then he added, for good measure, "BAH!"

It seemed like the airplane fell away from them, racing toward the horizon, as they hurtled toward the ground. The wind roared and Oliver kept shouting, at first with terror and then, suddenly, with glee. He didn't feel like he was falling at all.

He felt like he was flying.

With his mother behind him, in control of the parachute, strapped and buckled securely together, he actually had an amazing new thought, something he couldn't remember ever thinking before: his father was right.

Jumping out of an airplane was a lot of fun when you did it on purpose.

"Look!" his mother shouted in his ear. He looked up and saw the curve of the Earth, like the top of a big blue balloon, water and ice and sky and clouds arcing before him.

"Whoa!" he yelled, because what else was there to say?

Celia saw her brother and mother below.

"Ready?" her father yelled, but before she could say "No, I am certainly not ready to jump out of an airplane," her father jumped.

She wanted to frown or scream or complain about the noise, but she couldn't. She couldn't even wipe the grin off her face. It was amazing.

Suddenly, her father reached around and hugged her, pinning her arms to her sides and leaning forward. They shot downward like a bullet, racing straight for Oliver and her mother.

This time Celia found her scream. "AAH!"

She streaked past her brother with a *whoosh*. Oliver felt his arms pinned down to his sides.

"We're gonna get them!" his mother yelled, and they too were off, racing through the sky after his father and Celia.

While a family vacation to an amusement park or a nature hike is quite enjoyable, it must be said that nothing brings a family closer together than racing to the Earth at two hundred miles per hour. Dr. Navel would have liked to note, were he able to speak at this moment, that they were currently moving at the same speed as the peregrine falcon when it dives after its prey.

Oliver, at that moment, did not feel like a peregrine falcon diving after its prey. He tasted the bitter bite of adrenaline at the back of his mouth, and a tingle raced from his bellybutton up his spine. This wasn't fear or terror, but it wasn't bored or annoyed either. It didn't exactly feel good. It was dangerous and crazy and scary, but also . . . thrilling.

"Faster!" he yelled and straightened his body out as much as he could, which he noticed lowered the wind resistance against him and gave them some extra speed. They were catching up. They were gaining on Celia. Maybe he did feel a little like a peregrine falcon for just a second.

In a flash they shot past Celia. His mother let his arms go and they slowed beside his sister.

Oliver tried to stick his tongue out, but with his mouth open the wind grabbed his cheeks and they flapped like he was pressing them onto a window and blowing.

Celia laughed, and the wind pulled her mouth open in the same way. For a moment, all four of the Navels were diving together through the sky, laughing and making crazy windblown faces at each other.

Svalbard grew larger and larger beneath them. The ocean around it was a crackling sheet of ice, webbed with channels of water running in the cracks.

Dr. Navel tapped his wrist and gave a thumbs up. Claire Navel returned the thumbs up, and suddenly Oliver felt himself jerked back and up. There was a billowy *thump* as their parachute opened. They swirled and swooped and slowed. They weren't so much diving like falcons anymore. They were gliding.

But Celia and Dr. Navel below them were still diving. In fact, it looked more like they were just falling. They grew smaller and smaller as they tumbled toward the icy patch of land.

"Why aren't they opening their parachute?" Oliver yelled, but his mother couldn't hear him. Suddenly, the taste at the back of Oliver's mouth wasn't the metallic bite of adrenaline, but the acid taste of dread. Something had gone horribly wrong.

Dr. Navel pulled the rip cord.

Nothing happened. He pulled again, and still nothing.

He shook his head in disbelief. Of course they would have a problem now, just when he thought he was getting his daughter to enjoy a little excitement. He hoped Celia hadn't noticed there was a problem.

She had.

"Dad?" Celia yelled. "Daaad!"

He couldn't hear her. Svalbard had turned from a white speck in the ocean to an unforgiving expanse of rock rising up to flatten them.

"Open the chute!" Celia yelled. "Open it now!"

She should have known, she thought. Oliver would have added this to his list of rules. If you jump out of an airplane on TV, the parachute is always going to fail. Even if it almost never happens in real life, it always happens on TV. And that meant it would happen to Celia. Was that irony, Celia wondered, or just cruel fate?

Dr. Navel pulled the cord for the emergency parachute and it billowed and filled, slowing their fall. Celia exhaled with relief. Sometimes, she thought, having her dad around made things go a lot better than they did on TV.

They landed with a bump and skid, but they were safely on the ground. Only a few minutes had passed since they had jumped out of the airplane, but it felt like a lifetime.

Dr. Navel hauled in the parachute so the wind didn't lift them off the ground again. He unclipped his daughter. She stepped away from him and crossed her arms, giving him a withering glare.

"Good news!" Dr. Navel said. "It went better than our first skydive together, right?"

"I guess," said Celia, remembering their plane ride to Tibet when they fell out of an airplane with no parachutes and her father had been unconscious. Even with things going wrong, it *had* been more fun this time.

Now that they were on the ground and the thrill of the jump had worn off, she realized how cold it was. She shivered, and her father put his arm around her. They looked up at the sky together, watching as Oliver and his mother came down for a gentle landing.

"Your mother was always the better skydiver," Dr. Navel observed.

Oncc he was safely on the ground and unclipped from his mom, Oliver trotted over to Celia. Dr. Navel rushed over to his wife.

"We just went skydiving," Oliver said, studying her face to see how she felt about that.

"Yeah," said Celia, trying to do the same to him.

"It was . . . you know . . . ," Oliver said.

"Kind of fun?" said Celia.

"Yeah!" Oliver almost danced in place. "It was awesome. I felt like *Agent Zero*! I can't wait to tell Corey about it. I can't believe we raced in the air! I can't believe you had to open your emergency chute . . . I thought you were doomed. I mean, that's like a rule! It's crazy! I want to do it again!"

"Oliver," Celia stopped him. "Calm down. You sound like Dad."

That stopped him. He looked over at his father and mother, who were studying the parachute that didn't work and trying to figure out what went wrong.

"I guess I do," said Oliver. "I never liked excitement before."

"Me neither," said Celia. "What's happening to us?"

"I think we're getting old." Oliver sighed. "We're almost twelve. I guess pretty soon we'll like eating brussels sprouts and fried scorpions and going deep-sea diving like all the other old people."

"I don't think most old people like eating scorpions and going deep-sea diving," said Celia. "That's just Mom and Dad."

"They're so weird," agreed Oliver.

"It could be worse," said Celia.

"Yeah," said Oliver. "Brussels sprouts."

"No," said Celia. "Mom could still be missing."

"Oh yeah, that," said Oliver. "Right." He was still wondering how anyone could ever like brussels sprouts.

"Okay." Their mother came over to them. "If my bearings are correct, we're near the Danskøya research station."

Celia looked around. She didn't see anything that looked like a research station. She didn't see any signs of civilization at all. The ground was rocky and icy. Frozen glaciers loomed on the horizon and the light was dim, like twilight, and the temperature was dropping fast.

"Can we get there quickly?" Celia asked, her teeth starting to chatter with the cold.

"Oh, we'll have to," said her mother. "Otherwise we'll freeze to death in a matter of minutes."

Her mother wrapped the parachute around Celia's shoulders to give her some extra warmth. Oliver got the other one. They started to shuffle across the ice, looking like royalty trailing their robes behind them.

That made it quite easy for the grave robber in white camouflage to follow them from a distance so they would never see her coming. At least, not until it was too late.

15

WE SEE A DRAGON

THE ENTRANCE TO the research station was a mouth in the ice, an open tunnel supported by steel beams. Normally, Celia and Oliver would not have wanted to rush into a dark tunnel carved out of solid ice. As far as their rules went, there were certain to be unpleasant surprises in store for them, but in this case, it should be noted that they were the first inside, running through the ice and blustery wind for the promise of warmth. Celia didn't even make Oliver go first, although this time he wouldn't have minded.

Inside, the air hummed with the sound of machinery. The tunnel was carved directly in the permafrost, which was the layer of ground that was always frozen, even in the summer. There was a metal walkway down the middle where they walked, with lights hanging over it every few feet, but no railings. The walls had streaks of ice running through them, like layers of icing inside a cake. They could see a large steel door ahead that led deeper into the tunnel and there was an intercom box next to the door.

"Cozy," grumbled Celia.

"Why do they need such a heavy door?" Oliver wondered.

"Wouldn't want polar bears dropping in for a visit," their father said.

"And there are much older dangers than polar bears in the frozen realms of the north," their mother added.

"Why'd she have to say realms?" Oliver muttered. "It makes it sound so . . ."

"Enigmatic?" said Celia.

"Is that like mysterious?"

Celia nodded.

"Then, yeah. Enigmatic. She could have just said 'places' or something."

"She's an explorer," said Celia. As if that explained everything.

"That hum," said Oliver. "That sounds like air conditioning."

"It is," their mother said.

"What?" Celia wondered. "Who would turn on the air conditioning in a freezing cave?"

"If it gets too warm down here, the ice will melt and the ground will be too heavy. The tunnel would collapse, crushing the research station," their mother said.

"Oh," said Celia, pulling her parachute robe tighter around herself. She wiggled her toes and was happy to note that she could still feel them.

Dr. Navel hit the buzzer.

Nothing happened.

He hit it again.

No answer.

"Where is he?" Dr. Navel shook his head. "The researcher never leaves his post up here."

Oliver pushed on the big steel door and it creaked slowly open.

"Of course," he groaned. "Now I bet there will be something creepy on the other side."

"Why don't you go find out?" Celia suggested.

"Why do I have to go first?"

"I'm older," said Celia. "And anyway, that's your catchphrase." She shoved him through the door.

"Gah!" he screamed.

His sister and his parents rushed in after him to see Oliver crouched on the floor beneath a saber-toothed tiger.

"It's not alive, stupid." Celia shook her head. The tiger was half embedded in the ice of the wall and half dug out, so it looked like it was leaping. "It's, like, a fossil or something."

"I know that," said Oliver, standing up again.

"It's a perfectly preserved specimen," said Dr. Navel. "The saber-toothed tiger has been extinct for over ten thousand years. Who knows how long this one has been preserved in the permafrost?"

"Thirty-two thousand years," said Celia. She pointed to an information card next to it. "They're calling it a smilodon."

"That's from the ancient Greek for 'smile' and 'knife,'" their mother said.

"Knife smile," said Oliver with a gulp. "Nope, not creepy at all."

"Don't worry," Celia smirked. "I'll protect you from the extinct animals."

He stuck his tongue out at her.

"Come on," their mother called, and they continued into the cave. Dr. Navel stayed behind to study the smilodon in the ice.

"Extraordinary." He practically shoved his face into the creature's mouth. The twins imagined it must smell a lot like Sir Edmund's breath.

Farther down in the cave, where the air was warmer and the hum of the air conditioner even louder, their mother stopped in front of a row of bones sticking out of the wall. Each was about the size of a dinner plate. She pointed proudly at them.

"Look at this!" She smiled.

"It's bones," said Oliver.

"You know, guys," their mother said. "You can't just be couch potatoes forever."

"We're not couch potatoes," said Oliver.

"We're audiovisual enthusiasts," Celia corrected her mother.

"And I guess bones are cool," said Oliver.

His mother smiled. "These are dinosaur bones."

Oliver stepped closer.

"They are a hundred and fifty million years old," she added. "And they belong to the largest sea monster ever to have lived, the pliosaur. Some call it the Tyrannosaurus rex of the ocean. These bones here are just the vertebrae from the spine. Look."

She rushed deeper down into the cave and Oliver followed right behind her. The row of bones that made up the spine blossomed into a rib cage bigger than their living room at home, then long flippers that were taller than their mother, and then to a skull that was ten feet long with teeth the size of Oliver's arms.

"It is the largest and most complete reptile fossil ever found," Claire told her kids. "These were fierce hunters of the deep—sea dragons. This one sank into the mud when he died and was perfectly preserved. Look at the claws. This one was probably amphibious."

"That means he could go on land too," said Celia.

"I know what amphibious means," said Oliver. "Like a frog."

"Imagine when these dragons filled the oceans and wandered the earth." Their mother sighed, delighted.

"I'd rather not," said Oliver, who liked giant lizards even less than regular lizards, even if this giant lizard happened to be extinct.

"How do you know so much about this place?" wondered Celia.

"This is where your father and I met." Her mother smiled. "We were both doing research here and we fell in love digging for Viking gold. All we found were dragon bones," she sighed, "and each other."

"Ew," said Oliver. Imagining his parents being romantic was worse than getting eaten by a pliosaur.

"It's such a romantic place," she continued. "In the myths, dragons love gold, they can smell it, and we thought maybe the myths were based on these dragons. We could have stayed here searching for a long time."

"Why'd you leave?" Oliver wondered.

"You two were coming along." Their mother smiled. "But I always believed I'd be back. There's so much wonder here. So much unknown. The deeper explorers dig in the ice, the more remarkable species we find." She was almost breathless with excitement. "In Tibet they have discovered mammoth rhinoceroses, and here, a dragon."

"Mom," said Celia. "How is all this going to help us find Atlantis?"

"Well, I had hoped to discuss that with the researcher here, but the place seems to be empty."

"That's not a good sign," said Oliver.

"Where's Dad?" asked Celia.

"Oh, I'm sure he's just studying that fossil," said Claire. "Oggie? Ogden!"

"Oh no," said Oliver.

"Not good," said Celia.

"What's wrong?" Their mother turned back to them.

"We're in trouble," said Oliver.

"What do you mean?"

"It's about his rules," said Celia.

"They're not *my* rules," said Oliver. "They're just, like, *the* rules. Watch any movie. If you're in a creepy place and you call somebody's name and he doesn't come, well, you know something terrible is about to happen."

Their mother looked doubtful.

"He's right," said Celia. "This is always when something terrible happens."

"I'm sure your father just has his head stuck in the saber-toothed tiger's mouth," their mother said. "We're perfectly safe down here."

"See?" said Oliver. "Someone always says that too."

"Oggie?" their mother called again, worry starting to etch lines on her forehead.

"I'm here!" he called, coming slowly toward them.

"See?" said their mother. "Everything is fine."

"Not exactly," said another voice from behind their father. That's when their father stepped into view, his hands held high in the air. Behind him walked a woman in a white snowsuit and white wool cap. She had a snarl on her face and a pistol in her hand.

"Janice," whispered Celia.

"See?" whispered Oliver. He really hated being right about this sort of thing. Like all their enemies, from Ernest the celebrity impersonator to commercial breaks during their favorite shows, Janice McDermott—grave robber, thief, and mercenary—had a way of coming back over and over again.

16

WE DON'T MIND OUR MANNERS

SIR EDMUND'S PHONE rang. He let it ring while he studied the ancient map in front of him, the strange continents, the old Greek writing, the illustration of the dragon. He twirled his mustache and daydreamed about Atlantis.

The phone stopped ringing.

He looked up from the map to the portraits on his wall, heavy oil paintings of great leaders of the Council who came before him: Napoleon and Julius Caesar, Genghis Khan and Francisco Pizarro. Their grim visages looked down at him.

He smirked, because he would outdo them all.

The phone rang again and this time he answered.

"Tell me you have them," he said into the receiver without saying hello. We should not be surprised that a villain set on world domination would not place a high value on telephone manners.

He listened quietly for the answer to his question. His smile grew broader and broader as he heard Janice speak. When she was done, he did not answer immediately. Janice McDermott was a talented mercenary, which meant she sold her cruel set of skills—like grave robbing, thieving, and murdering—to whoever could pay her the most, and right now, Sir Edmund was paying her a lot. She was his employee and she could wait for his reply. Again, poor phone manners.

"You there? Hello?" Janice said. "Can you hear me now? I said that the Navels came here, just like you said they would. They've got no animals to help them out, no friends lurking in the shadows. They're all together and they're all under my control."

"I heard you," Sir Edmund said, standing up and resting his hand on the ancient rune stone of Nidhogg the dragon, which he now kept behind his desk. He couldn't read a word of the ancient language of the runes, but he liked to run his hand over it and know that it was priceless and that it was his.

One day, he believed, there would be monuments like this dedicated to Sir Edmund S. Titheltorpe-Schmidt III. Small though he was in height, he was grand in accomplishment. Now was the moment to complete his plans. Now was the moment to reach Atlantis and to claim the Lost Library. Now the world would be his to—

"Hello? Hello?" Janice's voice crackled over the phone line, cutting off his reverie.

Sir Edmund set the receiver down on the desk. He pressed a few buttons on his desk and the picture of Genghis Khan slid aside to reveal a screen with a picture of a Viking map of the north. The area of the North Pole was almost as unknown now as it was then, a frozen patch of ocean haunted by ghost-white polar bears and fields of treacherous ice. In Viking times, the only label for the upper reaches of the ice of the north was Asgard, the city of the gods at the top of a rainbow bridge. He zoomed in. He saw an illustration of a dragon, just like the one on Plato's map. The clues were all falling into place.

He pressed a button and the portrait of Genghis Khan slid back into place. He picked the phone up again.

"Edmund?" Janice was shouting. "Are you still there? Edmund?"

"It's *Sir* Edmund," he said. "Now quit shouting."

"What do you want me to do?" Janice said, her voice heavy with impatience.

"I'm on my way north. Keep them there. I have a delightful surprise."

He hung up the phone and set his palms flat on his desk, taking a deep breath and trying to keep from getting too excited. He wanted to squeal with glee, which would not suit a villain of his cunning and power.

Instead, he exhaled slowly.

He picked up the phone and dialed a number. When a gruff voice on the other end answered, Sir Edmund did not offer a greeting. "Tell the rest of the Council that the Navels fell into our trap and success is within our reach."

"It better be," said the voice. "Or you're finished. Their patience has worn out."

"Oh, don't go sweating through your little baseball cap. I know you want to take over the Council. I'm sorry to disappoint you."

"We'll see," the man on the phone said.

Sir Edmund wanted to stick his tongue out

and make barfing sounds, which also would not suit a villain of his cunning and power and perhaps would not have been very effective over the phone. Instead, he grunted and hung up.

He ran his fingers over the ancient map once more.

He would head off to Svalbard himself to claim his ultimate glory.

And, of course, get rid of the Navel family forever.

17

WE GET SOME TV TIME

JANICE KEPT ONE hand on her pistol as she sipped a steaming cup of hot chocolate. The Navels stood against the wall opposite, their hands above their heads, just as she had ordered.

She leaned back in her chair, which blocked the only door out of the small dining room where the researcher used to sit and eat his lonely meals. Before he'd been kidnapped, that is. It was a heavy steel door, strong enough to keep out any stray polar bears that might somehow find their way past the heavy outer doors to the research station. It looked strong enough to keep out a lot more than bears. It could probably keep out a pliosaur like the one fossilized in the cave outside. Not that anyone wanted to find out.

Janice put her feet up on the table, her wet shoes dripping on the research papers and maps of glaciers that had been left lying about. On the wall behind her, bright posters gave safety advice like: *If your hands are feeling numb, don't be dumb, warm them, chum! Keep bear protection with you at times!* and the obvious, *Why not stay inside?*

"Duh," Oliver muttered as he read.

Celia stared down the barrel of Janice's gun, defiant, plotting a way out of yet another mess her parents had gotten them into. Oliver licked his lips and stared at the steaming mug of hot chocolate, defiant, plotting a way to get some of it for himself.

Here, in the far north, they had no hope of being rescued by the sudden appearance of their pet lizard or monkey or chicken. Corey Brandt and Professor Rasmali-Greenberg were long gone in the airplane with their friends, and no other children from some distant tribe could find them here. No one lived this far north. There would be no *deus ex machina* for Oliver and Celia this time.

"I've spoken to Edmund," Janice said. "And he is very impressed that you were able to find your way here without a map. He sends his compliments."

"We don't want his compliments," their mother snapped.

"Listen, Janice," said Dr. Navel. "What do you

want Oliver and Celia for? They're only children. At least let them go."

"Ha!" Janice laughed. "Your children have proven far more dangerous to our efforts than you have. We're much more likely to keep them and let you go."

"No way," said Oliver.

"I was just making a point," said Janice. "I'm not letting anyone go. In fact, I have a much more interesting idea."

"And what's that?" Dr. Navel sneered at her.

She smiled and stood. She sauntered over to a control panel in the corner of the room. She hit a few buttons. The loud hum of the air conditioner stopped. Then she shot the panel several times.

"Aack!" They couldn't cover their ears fast enough. The loud shots from her gun in such a small space rattled their eardrums.

"That is not proper firearm safety!" Dr. Navel shouted.

"It's going to start to get warm in here," said Janice. "And as it does, the ice will melt and the ground will get softer and collapse right onto this research station. Maybe in a few thousand years, some scientists will find your fossils down here near those old dragon bones and wonder what sort of strange creatures would have perished just sitting around in front of a television. A fitting way for two couch potatoes to meet their end, I think?"

"We're not couch potatoes," said Oliver.

"We're audiovisual enthusiasts," Celia explained again.

"Wait," said Oliver. "There's a TV in here?" He glanced to the side and saw a small TV screen in an odd console sitting in the corner.

"Enjoy it," said Janice. "It will be your last chance. None of you will be getting in our way again."

"Don't be a fool, Janice," Claire Navel warned. "You know you can't trust Sir Edmund. If you let us go, I'm sure we can work out a reward."

"Like that's going to happen," scoffed Janice. "Watching this cave collapse on you and your snot-nosed kids is my reward. Well, that and twenty-five million dollars."

"We're not snot-nosed kids," said Oliver, wiping his nose on his sleeve just to be sure.

"We're snot-nosed tweens," said Celia. "I mean, er, we're not snot-nosed anythings!"

"Money will be worthless when Sir Edmund brings ruin to us all," said their mother. "Do you realize what he has planned? If he can find the Lost Library, he will try to raise Atlantis. It'll bring unimaginable destruction to the world. A new continent rising, geological disaster, floods and fires and famine."

"Fantasy." Janice laughed. "It's all fantasy to me. Money is real and I'll get plenty of it. Revenge is real and I'm getting that right now."

"You're a monster," said Dr. Navel.

Janice shrugged. "As delightful as it is to sit with you, I'd rather watch ice melt. Sir Edmund is on his way and I can't wait to show him that I have finally gotten rid of you. Enjoy your time together."

She strolled out of the small room and stopped at the door. She turned back around and snatched her hot chocolate off the table and took it with her as slammed the door on her way out.

"Darn!" Oliver kicked the table leg, his hot chocolate hopes dashed.

They heard chains rattle and locks snapping shut.

Dr. Navel rushed to the door to pound on it, but to no avail. Janice did not open the door again. "Well, this is a pickle." He leaned back against the door and rubbed his eyes. "What now?"

"We could watch the TV," suggested Oliver.

His parents looked at him with mouths agape. Who would want to watch television at a time like this?

"What?" said Oliver.

"He's right," said Celia. "It beats just watching the ice melt."

18

WE WATCH ICE MELT

THEIR PARENTS WATCHED the walls drip with melting ice.

"Let us out! Let us out!" Dr. Navel pounded on the door again.

"She isn't going to let us out, dear," said Claire. "She probably can't even hear us."

As the air in the research station warmed with every breath they took, beads of condensation formed, like on the outside of cold glass of lemonade on a hot summer day. Oh, how Oliver and Celia wished they were drinking lemonade on a hot summer day instead of being trapped in an underground Arctic research station, watching the ceiling sag under its own weight! The melting ice formed puddles by the walls, dripped onto the table, and ran down the steel door that sealed them inside the room.

The twins fiddled with the little TV in the corner. It had a lot of strange knobs and dials and switches, but they couldn't figure out how to turn it on.

"You can use the remote if you want," said Celia.

Oliver rushed over to the backpack, glad he got to be in control of the universal remote control for once. He pressed a button and the TV in the corner hummed to life.

"I can't believe you two can watch TV right now," said their father.

"It's calming," said Oliver.

"TV has helped us out before," added Celia. "And it's more fun than banging on the door."

However, the TV was not going to be more fun than banging on the door, because it wasn't a regular TV. It didn't get any channels at all. It was, however, going to helpful.

It was a security monitor and it showed them an image of themselves standing in front of the TV in the room they were in. They looked over their shoulders and saw the security camera mounted in the corner, pointing down at them.

Oliver waved and watched himself wave on the TV.

Celia snatched the remote from his hand and changed the channel.

"Hey, I was watching that," he objected.

Their parents came over to see.

Channel two showed the tunnel on the other side of the door, where the saber-toothed tiger and the skeleton of the prehistoric dragon were frozen into the wall. She hit the button again and saw a snow-covered helicopter pad on the roof of the station. The next channel showed the front, where Janice had set up a tent with lights and a heater hooked up to her snowmobile for electricity.

"Why's she camping out front?" Oliver wondered.

"She's probably waiting around to watch us get smushed," said Celia. "That's her idea of entertainment."

"She's probably waiting for Sir Edmund," said Dr. Navel. "And to watch us get smushed," he added.

Celia changed the channel again and they saw a kennel on the other side of the research station. There were half a dozen doghouses and a storage shed, all surrounded by a fence to keep the dogs in and polar bears out.

"Dogs," said Oliver.

"That's it!" said their mother. "That's how we're going to beat Sir Edmund to the North Pole! On a dogsled!"

"Sure," said Celia. "But how are we going to get out of this room?"

"Hmm." The room fell silent. Only the sound of dripping water marked the passing minutes.

Oliver was dancing from foot to foot, excited about riding on a dogsled. Or he had to pee. Maybe it was both.

Celia started to sweat. She couldn't believe how hot she was in the Arctic Circle. She tugged at her collar and slumped against the wall. She groaned and stared at the water dripping from the ceiling. "It's so hot," she complained. "I miss the air conditioner."

"Oh, Celia!" Her mother jumped up. "You're a genius!"

"She is?" said Oliver.

"I am?" said Celia. "I mean, yes, I am . . . but . . . uh . . . why?"

"The air conditioner isn't running!" said her mother, stating the most obvious fact in the world. The air conditioner not running was exactly the thing that was going to get them smushed.

The twins watched their mother drag a chair across the room and climb up to the air conditioning vent. She undid the screws and looked in. She banged on the sides.

"It's big enough for the two of you to go through, get to the tunnel, and open the door from the other side," she told them.

"Do we have to?" said Celia.

"Do you want to be smushed under a thousand tons of ice and rock until some future explorer digs you up and finds your bones?"

"I guess I'll go first." Oliver sighed and stood.

Dr. Navel hoisted Oliver up into the vent.

"Hold on." Their mother caught Celia by the foot before she climbed in. She fidgeted with the gold ring she wore, the one engraved with the symbol of the Mnemones. "Take this." She pulled the ring off her finger and pressed the metal into Celia's hand. She looked her daughter square in the eyes. "Just in case something happens."

An understanding passed between them. Celia knew that if something went wrong, she had to go on to find the Lost Library and save the day and keep Oliver from getting eaten by a polar bear.

Celia's mother knew that if her children succeeded, they would be getting televisions in their rooms and she would stay at home to watch with them, never leaving them for another crazy adventure. Before she knew what she was doing, Celia found herself hugging her mother.

"Let's hope it doesn't come to that," her mother whispered.

Inside the vent Oliver wondered why it was taking Celia so long to get up there. He didn't like how narrow the space was. His breath hung heavy in front of him. The air duct was just wide enough for him the crawl forward on his elbows and knees, but not really to look behind him or to turn around. There was no going back. He heard the loud banging as his sister was hoisted in behind him. They clunked along single file through the cool metal air duct.

"This reminds me of going through that tunnel at the Explorers Club when we were going to run away," said Oliver. "Before we found Mom again."

"Yeah," said Celia.

"Do you ever regret not running away?" he asked Celia.

She thought about all the times they'd fallen out of airplanes or been attacked by wild animals or chased by murderous thugs. She thought about meeting Corey Brandt and seeing the Amazon and the open sea and spending time with her whole family together. She thought about all the TV she'd missed. "I dunno," she said.

"I'm glad we didn't run away," said Oliver.

"I guess if I had to not run away from a family, this one's not so bad to not run away from," Celia said.

"Huh?" Oliver had no idea what she was talking about, but she didn't have a chance to explain. He stopped suddenly at another vent and Celia bumped into him from behind.

"Ow!" he said. He jostled the vent cover but couldn't get it open. The screws wouldn't budge. He knocked it and it shook a little, but it didn't open.

"Hurry up," said Celia. "My legs are getting a cramp!"

"I'm trying," he said.

"Try harder!" said Celia and she shoved him again. His head hit the vent and it flexed. He looked at it again. He exhaled.

"Do that again," he said.

"What? Yell at you?"

"Shove me."

"You want me to shove you?"

"Yeah." He sighed.

"Are you sure? You always complain when I shove you. Do you have a toxic parasite or something?"

"No, just shove me," he said again.

Celia shrugged and threw herself forward into Oliver's back. With a thud from Oliver's head and a clatter of metal, the vent burst open and the twins spilled out into the tunnel next to a row of lockers down the hall from the room their parents were trapped in.

They stood and brushed themselves off.

Celia glanced up and down the tunnel.

"What are you doing?" wondered Oliver.

"I want to make sure Janice hasn't come back inside."

"Good idea," said Oliver, who was glad Celia thought of things like that.

"The coast is clear." Celia turned back to her brother. "Let's go rescue Mom and Dad."

"As usual," Oliver mumbled in reply.

19

WE CAN'T GO ON, WE'LL GO ON

THEY MADE THEIR way back to the heavy steel door. They knew their parents were waiting anxiously on the other side. Oliver kept a lookout for Janice while Celia studied the chains.

"There are too many of them," she said. She yanked on one of the giant padlocks. It was almost too heavy for her to move. And it was only one of five holding the heavy steel chains Janice had wrapped around the door handles. They couldn't pry them loose.

"There's no way to get Mom and Dad out?"

"There's no way through this door," said Celia. "And the vent's too small."

"Let's see what they think we should do," suggested Oliver. He hit a button on the intercom next to the door. "Uh . . . hi," he said. "Oliver here."

"Are you all right?" his father's voice crackled through the speaker. "We started to worry."

"We're fine," Celia said, pressing her face to the microphone.

"Can you get the door open?" their mother's voice crackled through.

"It's chained!" said Celia. "We can't open it."

"Check for chain cutters in the supply lockers," their father suggested.

Oliver rushed back to the lockers and started rummaging. There was a lot of fancy cold-weather gear, but nothing that could cut chains. He ran back, out of breath, and delivered the bad news.

"What do we do?" Celia called into the intercom.

Silence hung heavy in the air. They waited for their parents to answer.

"I think you know," their mother's voice came through at last.

"She does?" said Oliver.

"I do?" said Celia.

"You do," said their mother.

Celia's shoulders sagged. She looked at her

brother, who watched her, wide eyed and expectant. She was three minutes and forty-two seconds
older. She felt the weight of her age and responsi-
bility heavy on her now.

"I do." She sighed. "Mom wants us to sneak
out, take the dogsled, and get to the North Pole
before Sir Edmund."

"What?" said Oliver. "She does?"

"Yeah," said Celia.

"I do," their mother's voice crackled sadly.

"But . . . but . . . we're just kids," said Oliver.

"We're tweens," said Celia.

"You're tweens," their mother said at the same
time. "And I believe you can do anything."

"But what about you? We can't leave you and
Dad here!" Oliver objected.

"The Lost Library is more important than
your father and me," she said.

"Not to us," said Oliver.

It was their mother's turn to feel the silence
heavy in the air.

"We'll be fine here for a while. There's food
and water in the fridge in here, and it will take a
few days for this place to be in danger of collapsing. We'll figure something out."

"We'll try harder," said Oliver. "We'll break you out! We can't go alone!"

"We can't break them out." Celia pulled Oliver's hand off the button so their parents couldn't hear. "We have to go on alone. If we find Atlantis maybe we can trade with Sir Edmund for the Lost Library. He frees our parents and lets us go, and he gets what he wants."

"But Mom would never let us do that," said Oliver. "What about Sir Edmund causing fire and flood and famine and geo-whatever disaster, like she said?"

"You believe in all that?"

Oliver shrugged. "I believe in a lot of stuff."

Celia just gave him her look, her long look for a long time, and eventually Oliver shook his head. "Fine," he said. "We'll do it."

"Good," said Celia, glad that she could still get her brother to do what he needed to do without her needing to say anything. "Now you have to go back through the vents and get our backpack. We'll never find our way without the journal and the compass."

"Why do I have to go back?"

"One of us has to get the cold-weather clothes

together so we don't freeze to death and keep a look out in case Janice comes back."

"Why not me?" said Oliver.

"I thought you might want to hug Mom and Dad good-bye," Celia suggested.

"Yeah, I do . . ." Oliver kicked his toes into the floor. "Don't you?"

"I'm gonna do it when we get back," said Celia. She didn't want to tell him about the moment she'd had with her mother or about the Mnemones' ring. It seemed somehow private.

"Oliver's coming back to get our stuff," she said into the intercom. "And then we'll go save the world."

"See you soon, honey," her mother and father said. "We love you."

"Uh-huh," Celia replied. "We'll leave you the remote control," she said. She couldn't think of anything else to say.

20

WE MUSH-MUSH

WHEN OLIVER RETURNED with the back-pack, his face was streaked with sweat and maybe, thought Celia, a tear or two. She didn't ask. He'd never admit it, and anyway, that was his business. She had raided the lockers and it was time to get bundled up in cold-weather gear.

All of it was much too large for them.

To get their pants and sleeves to fit and to seal them against the cold required the aggressive application of duct tape. They had floppy wool hats under their oversized hoods and shiny space-blanket strips covering their faces and necks. Goggles protected their eyes.

As they crept back through the tunnel toward the freezing arctic air, they looked more like alien explorers rising from the center of the earth than two eleven-and-half-year-olds going for a reluctant walk in the snow.

Celia glanced sadly at the thermometer by the mouth of the cave, which told the outside temperature: $-19°$ F.

She thought about the safety poster in the room they had escaped: *Why not stay inside?*

Oliver must have been thinking about it too, because they sighed in unison just before they stepped out into the biting cold. Janice's tent was a glowing bubble in the snow, but it was zipped up tight. They could make out her silhouette against the fabric. She couldn't see out, and they could hear her singing the theme song to *World's Best Rodeo Clown* to herself.

"Red noses ride! Red noses ride! Hi-ho! Hi-ho! Hi-ho, Red Noses, put on your big shoes and riiide!"

The twins glanced at each other and thought about trying to surprise her and get the keys to all those locks. When they looked back, they saw that she was holding her pistol and twirling it. Trying to get the jump on her would be way too dangerous. They'd stick to Plan A. Travel to the North Pole by themselves and save the world.

When they thought about it, Plan A was pretty dangerous too.

They snuck around to the back of the research station, creeping low and staying close to the snowy walls. They saw the bear-proof fence and the rows of doghouses and supply sheds for the kennel, just like they'd seen it on the security monitor.

"Well, up you go," said Celia.

"You sure the fence isn't electric?" asked Oliver.

Celia bent down and made a quick snowball. She raised her arm and threw it. Oliver ducked and the snowball hit the fence, breaking apart.

"What'd you do that for?" Oliver demanded.

"The fence would have sizzled if it was still on," said Celia.

"You could have warned me first."

"But that wouldn't have been any fun." She smiled, but Oliver couldn't see it under her scarf. She couldn't see him stick out his tongue under his.

He scurried up the icy chain link. It was so cold that his gloves stuck to it as he climbed. He swung his legs over the top and dropped down into the snow on the other side with soft crunch. He felt like *Agent Zero* breaking into a secret Arctic base. He looked through the fence at Celia and gave a thumbs up.

"Watch out behind you!" she warned.

Oliver turned just in time to see six big Siberian huskies, white like wolves, come charging out of their doghouses and race toward him, howling and barking.

"Gah!" He jumped up the fence to climb back over—he didn't know how long it had been since someone had fed the dogs and he had no desire to become dog food—but they were too fast for him.

"Shh!" Celia warned. If her brother was about to be torn apart by dogs, she didn't want Janice coming out to shoot her too.

The first dog to reach Oliver jumped up and caught the back of his jacket in his teeth, pulling Oliver to the ground. Another big dog put his massive paw on Oliver's chest so he couldn't get up, and then the other dogs rushed in to attack.

"Don't eat me!" Oliver tried to get his hands up to protect his face, but it was too late. He felt a warm wet nose knock his goggles off and then a big wet tongue licked from his chin to his forehead. Soon the other dogs joined in, covering him in licks, nuzzling and rolling about on the snow next to him. Ever since the researcher had been kidnapped, no one had played with them. Dogs, even giant Siberian huskies trained to work, need to be played with.

Once he realized he wasn't going to be eaten, he wriggled out from underneath the dogs and got up to open the gate. As soon as he swung it open, Celia received just as excited a greeting from the sled dogs. They knocked her off her feet and licked her face until it was soaked and the doggy drool had frozen.

"Gross," she said, wiping her face on her sleeve, but smiling just the same. It felt good to get normal affection from a normal pet. They'd only ever had exotic lizards and fierce monkeys and, lately, one ex-pirate chicken named Dennis.

The twins scurried over to the supply shed and slipped inside, the dogs wagging their tails and heeding Celia's constant warnings to shush.

Inside, they saw a state-of-the-art fiberglass dogsled, already loaded with supplies for an expedition. The researcher must have been planning to go somewhere before Janice kidnapped him.

"Hey cool," said Oliver, lifting the tarp on the sled. "He packed cheese puffs! And freeze-dried soup!"

"It's too cold for soup," said Celia. "Let's drag this outside and get the dogs hooked up."

There was one thick rope with six smaller ones branching off the front of it, and each of those ropes had a harness on the end of it. As Oliver went around to pull from the front, Celia grabbed a canister marked BEAR REPELLENT and slipped it into her pocket with her mother's gold ring. The she grabbed the ropes beside her brother and pulled. The twins heaved and hauled to get the sled outside, while the dogs watched them with their heads cocked to the side and their piercing blue eyes wide.

"Aren't they supposed to pull the sled?" Oliver grunted.

"We've got to get them into the harnesses first," said Celia, giving the sled one more tug before flopping down into the snow to rest.

"How are we gonna do that?" Oliver wondered.

The twins looked up at the dogs. The dogs looked down at the twins. Neither side moved.

"Go!" Celia tried.

The dogs didn't move.

"Hut! Hut! Hut!" Oliver tried.

The dogs still didn't move.

"It's not football," said Celia.

Celia tried giving them her "do what I tell you" look, but it didn't work. She threw her arms in the air. Siberian huskies were harder to control than younger brothers.

"Well, this is even worse than being stuck inside," said Oliver. "I need a snack."

"That's it!" Celia hopped off the snow and rummaged on the sled. She pulled out a bag of cheese puffs and held it up.

"They can't have those," said Oliver.

"You don't think dogs eat cheese puffs?"

"Everyone eats cheese puffs!" said Oliver. "But we need those for ourselves!"

Celia shook her head at him. "There's plenty to go around." She ripped open the bag and the dogs immediately snapped to attention. They bounced over to her and sat. One by one Oliver hooked them into the harnesses and Celia rewarded them with a handful of cheese puffs.

When they were done Oliver turned to her, as eager as a puppy. She gave him a handful of cheese puffs too.

There was enough room on top of the sled for one person to sit with the supplies while the other person stood with one foot on each of the runners at the back of the sled, holding the handlebars. That person would be the "musher," who steered the sled and kept them going by calling out "Mush! Mush!"

"You can go first," said Celia, climbing onto the sled with her backpack.

For once, Oliver didn't complain about being made to go first. Celia knew he wouldn't. She could tell that he was excited about driving a dogsled, and that suited her just fine. She was looking forward to putting her feet up and going for a ride.

"So, uh," said Oliver. "Where do we go?"

Celia sighed. "I guess we look in the journal." She rummaged in her backpack and pulled out Percy Fawcett's journal.

"You really think that book can help us?"

"Listen." She read aloud, *"I begin my journey in the frozen north. I am gripped, I admit, by fear of what lies beyond. Will I be pulled off course by drifting ice? Will I meet the dragons of old? I cannot know."*

"Dragons?" Oliver swallowed. "That's not real, right?"

"Shh," said Celia. She continued, *"But I will follow the compass, and I shall prevail; no explorer, even one greater than I, should he exist, could follow this path I take. I shall be the last."*

"So what? So this guy was really full of himself," said Oliver.

"The greatest explorers shall be the least," said Celia. "That was our prophecy. So we can follow his path."

Oliver looked doubtful.

"Also, we have his compass," Celia added.

She rummaged around in their backpack and pulled out the small brass compass with the initials P.F. on the back. She held it flat in her hand. Instead of an *N* where north was on most compasses, it pointed to the symbol of a key, the Mnemones' symbol, and it would lead them as far north as a person could go in the world: the North Pole.

She handed the compass to Oliver. "Don't lose it," she said.

He squeezed it in his hand. She raised her eyebrows at him. Oliver had a way of losing things.

"I won't lose it!" Oliver grumbled.

"Don't."

"I won't!"

"You won't?"

"I won't!"

"Don't."

Oliver rolled his eyes at her, then he looked at the dogs. He felt his heart beat faster. The dogs looked back at him expectantly. The lead dog let out an eager bark, which the other dogs quickly copied, and soon it became a canine chorus of howls.

Oliver felt that same thing he felt when he was skydiving with his mother. Not safe or even comfortable, but happy in way he'd never felt, even during a special *Agent Zero* presented with limited commercial interruption by Cheese Puffs Brand Cheese Stumps. He wondered if Corey Brandt was back in Hollywood yet, and who he was going to get to play Oliver in the movie. If it weren't for the danger they were all in and the fate of the world resting on their tiny shoulders, he might even be enjoying himself.

"You know what to say?" asked Celia.

"Oh yeah," said Oliver with a grin. "I've almost memorized every episode of *Extreme Grandma Races.*"

Celia rolled her eyes.

"Mush! Mush!" Oliver shouted, and the dogs turned and took off, pulling the sled through the gate with a wild lurch.

"Aack! Eeek!" Celia gripped the sled, but her scream was mixed with laughter. Oliver leaned to the side and the dogs turned with him. Celia laughed again. "You drive like a lunatic!" she shouted, but not unkindly.

"It's my first time!" Oliver called back. He straightened the sled and blew out a frosty breath. Celia looked toward the horizon at the top of the world and shoved her hand into her pocket, feeling to make sure her mother's gold ring was still there.

"We'll be back," she whispered, because that was just the sort of vow that heroes made before they set out on an adventure. She hoped, even more than usual, that she was right.

21

WE ABSQUATULATE

CELIA LEANED BACK on the sled as they slid quietly across the ice. If she didn't think too much about the danger their parents faced or the terrible ordeal that lay ahead, she could almost enjoy herself.

Oliver was thinking the same thing as he held the handlebars and practiced leaning from side to side to steer the dogs.

"Mush! Mush!" he repeated and the dogs picked up speed. The freezing wind bit into the tiny part of his face that was exposed. He pulled up his scarf all the way to his goggles and felt pretty cozy.

On the horizon, jagged black mountains jutted into the sky. In front of them, the ice was smooth and hard and the dogs avoided any obstacles with ease.

Mushing wasn't so bad, he thought. It was even fun to say.

"Mush!" he said again, and the dogs barked cheerfully in reply.

Celia quickly grew bored riding on the sled, staring at the unchanging landscape. She pulled out the beat-up leather journal again and flipped through it. She flipped past the drawings of El Dorado and the Amazon, past the explorer's early notes, toward the end of his search where he'd drawn the pictures of the tree and the monsters and the man who looked like Santa Claus.

All lost places are the same lost places, the explorer had written. *As all lost souls are the same lost souls. The desire to be found burns in all of us.*

"What's that supposed to mean?" said Celia, flipping more pages. She read below a picture of Santa Claus: *Odin, god of battle, wisdom, and prophecy, ruler of the godly city of Asgard, crossed the rainbow bridge to Yggdrasil and hung himself upon it. Nine days he hung on the World Tree, as Ratatosk the squirrel hurled insults and Nidhogg the dragon gnawed at the roots. Odin looked to all the world below in all directions and saw all things to come for men and gods. He would be swallowed in the battle at the end of time but he would come back again and again. Time is a circle.*

"I think we aren't really looking for Santa Claus," said Celia.

"Just because you don't believe in him doesn't mean I have to stop," said Oliver.

"No," said Celia. "What I mean is, we're looking for Odin. Who is the same as Santa Claus. It's like reincarnation in Tibet. All things come back again and again. Time is a circle."

"Are you okay?" said Oliver. "You sound like an explorer."

Celia didn't answer her brother. She just studied the picture of the bearded man, ruler of a city called Asgard. Her mother had said that was the same as Atlantis. She studied the pictures of a buck-toothed squirrel and a dragon. She really didn't want to run into any of them. They were all just stories, right?

"Hey look," said Oliver.

"I'm thinking," said Celia. Her parents had never told her that explorers had to do so much reading.

"Just look up," he urged her.

"I'm trying to figure out where we're going," she said. "This book could help us."

"Just look up for a second."

"Fine, what is it?" Celia looked up from the journal and gasped at the sky.

Green ribbons of the aurora borealis, the northern lights, waved at them from the twilight. Ancient Vikings thought the northern lights were flashes of light shining off the armor of the Valkyries, Odin's maidens who ruled over the field of battle.

Oliver and Celia knew that the northern lights were caused by charged particles hitting the atmosphere. They'd seen *Wally Worm's Science Sensation.* Educational programming was dull, but they sure did learn a lot from it.

Not on purpose, of course.

"It's like a nature show," Oliver marveled.

"Madam Mumu was right," said Celia. "Wow."

Oliver craned his head back to stare at the light show above and watched as it twinkled and waved in the sky, pink and green reflecting off the white and blue ice.

"Watch out!" Celia shouted.

"What?" Oliver looked down. "Aack!" he screamed.

The dogs were running straight toward a crack in the ice, too wide to jump, a deep crevasse with glistening white sides and sharp edges.

"Tell them to turn!" Celia yelled.

"I'm trying!" said Oliver, pulling on the ropes. "Mush! Mush!"

The dogs sped up.

"That's not it!"

"I don't speak dog!"

He heaved the sled to the side and leaned with his whole body. The dogs yipped and barked as they turned along the edge of the crack at the last moment. Their legs didn't slip at all, but the sled swung with the momentum and the back runners slipped into the open air. Oliver, standing on the runners, lost his footing and dropped off the back, hanging from the sled by his hands. The compass clattered away into the cold water. His legs kicked helplessly above the frozen abyss.

"Don't let me fall!" Oliver yelled. "Mush! Mush!"

Celia dove across the back of the sled to grab her brother's arms. Ice and snow kicked up around them.

The dogs charged forward, struggling to pull the sled back onto solid ground. They strained, Celia pulled, and the sled rose and straightened away from the crack.

Oliver slumped over the handlebars, out of breath. They were moving smoothly again. The dogs panted and slowed to a trot. Oliver was panting too. On the plus side, he didn't really feel cold anymore. He was sweating inside his snowsuit.

"Let's not do that again," said Celia.

Oliver did not disagree. He swallowed hard. On the plus side, he was still alive. On the minus side, he'd lost the compass, just like Celia said he would. If they didn't get lost and freeze to death, she'd probably kill him as soon as she found out. Or she'd give him one of those "told you so" looks. Those were almost worse than dying.

"Mush." He sighed. The dogs gave him a long look, but didn't speed up. "Lazy dogs," he muttered.

"That's what people say about us," said Celia.

Oliver frowned at her. He looked back at the dogs. He felt bad for making them work so hard. But he felt bad about making himself work so hard too.

"Sorry, guys," he muttered. "I don't want to be here either, but we've got to keep going."

"Are you talking to the dogs?" said Celia.

"I'm building trust," said Oliver. "Like on *Dog University*."

"They can't understand you," said Celia.

"Dogs understand people," said Oliver. "Professor Pup says so."

"Professor Pup is made up for TV."

"So now you don't believe in Santa Claus or Professor Pup?"

"I *believe* my hands are numb and my toes are numb. I *believe* this whole thing is really dumb, but I'm doing it anyway because this journal says we have to find the city of Asgard, which will be Atlantis, in which will be hidden the Lost Library of Alexandria, and we need it to save Mom and Dad."

She held up the leather journal and waved it in the air.

"You're just making it more confusing by reading that book," said Oliver.

"It's not confusing," she told him. She took a deep breath and let out a river of words. "The Lost Library was hidden in Atlantis by the explorer who wrote this journal. Atlantis is really in the North Pole, the North Pole is the home of Santa Claus, Santa Claus is Saint Nicholas but also the Norse god Odin, Odin lived in a secret city called Asgard, but Asgard was destroyed sometime long, long ago (just like Atlantis because they're the same place), and we're here to find the ruins of that city buried in the ice so we can trade for Mom and Dad and Sir Edmund can use the Lost Library to raise Atlantis and rule the world. See?"

"Duh," said Oliver.

"You understand now?" Celia asked.

"I said duh, didn't I?"

"I just don't want to have to explain it again."

"I've got a brain," said Oliver. "I watch as much educational programming as you."

"Do not."

"Do too."

"Do not."

"Do too."

"What's the definition of *absquatulate*?"

"Uh . . ."

"See? If you *actually* paid attention when we watched educational programming, you would know that ab-squat-choo-late means to leave in a hurry. *Talking to you is not so great, it's time you must absquatulate*," she sang, imitating Wally the Word Worm's puppet voice.

"Whatever," said Oliver, looking back to the dogs. "Mush! Mush! Mush!"

With a loud sigh, the lead dog started to pull.

The others resisted a moment and then joined in, and once again the sled started moving. Oliver tried to guess which way they had been heading before. He still didn't want to tell his sister that he'd lost the compass, although the longer he waited, the worse it would be when she found out. Maybe he wouldn't need to tell her at all. Maybe the dogs would just know which way was north and they'd get there before Celia figured out that Oliver had screwed everything up, just like she said he would.

He was glad she couldn't see his face. She'd know right away that something was wrong. The trouble with having a twin sister was that you couldn't hide anything from her.

"Mush!" he said again, his voice cracking slightly with nerves. Celia didn't seem to notice.

It was a good thing that the twins decided to absquatulate when they did, because at that moment, across a thousand yards of ice, a polar bear stirred, smelling the scent of dogs and humans on the wind. It sniffed the air and began to follow the scent, with just one polar bear thought thrumming through its polar bear brain: dinner.

22

WE CLIMB THE OCEAN

THE SLED STOPPED in front of a giant wall of ice, five times as tall as Oliver and Celia. The dogs rested. The twins got off the sled and studied the barrier that stretched as far as they could see in both directions.

"It's like giants built a wall to keep people out," said Oliver.

"There is no such thing as giants," said Celia. She flipped through the book. She found the part she was looking for and read it out loud. *"There is a place in the far north where the land ends and the frozen ocean begins. A great wall of ice, at least twenty feet high, marks the border. It is a frozen wave, crashing ashore in slow motion. The ice floes beyond grind and crash into one another, pressing upward, forming great ridges, ever shifting, mountains of ice raised and torn down—moment to moment, day to day—so the landscape is never the same twice. Every explorer in*

the Arctic sees a new place, one that has never been
seen before, one that will never be seen again."

"Huh?" said Oliver.

"This is the ocean," said Celia, putting her hand on the ice. "It's just frozen. But it's moving."

"Great," said Oliver. "But how do we get over it? I don't think it's just going to move out of the way."

From within the ice came a groaning, the pressure of the entire frozen ocean pushing against the land. A boulder of snow tumbled down the side. The dogs whimpered, eager to run but frightened of the grinding and crashing in front of them.

"We'll have to climb," said Oliver. "And then we'll haul the dogs up one by one. And then we'll all pull up the sled."

Celia didn't answer. She knew they weren't strong enough to lift even one of the dogs, let alone all of them and the sled loaded with supplies. "I want to look in the journal one more time," she said.

"You and that book!" Oliver complained. "That book is just making this adventure more and more like school! Put it away! Let's climb!"

"We can't climb," said Celia.

"Just because you hate climbing doesn't mean we don't have to do it!"

"You hate climbing too."

"Not all the time."

"Name one time you've liked climbing." Celia crossed her arms and waited. She tapped her foot in the snow. The wind howled.

Oliver couldn't think of a time. He really did hate climbing. "Fine," he said. "You have a better idea?"

"Listen." Celia read aloud from the journal again. *"To the edge of the land now, the great wall of ice is before me, and I hesitate. The pressure ridge rises higher than I or my sled can go, and alone I will not be able get the dogs over. I must find a way up soon, before the polar bear stalking me makes its attack."*

"Polar bear?" Oliver glanced over his shoulder. He didn't believe in dragons, but he knew polar bears were real. He also knew they were some of the meanest, fiercest, most powerful predators in the world. He did not want to sit around waiting to become dinner for one. All he saw behind them, however, was an endless field of white.

"That's not the point," said Celia. "He couldn't lift his sled either, so he went to find a way up. If he found one, so can we. Come on!"

She jumped onto the sled. "Mush! Mush!" she called and the dogs started off along the wall.

"Hey, wait up! That's my job!" Oliver jumped on the runners again, nudging Celia out of the way. She climbed back to the front to sit down and ride.

"What's that?" Celia pointed. Up ahead, they could see big lumps in the ice, with bits of petrified wood sticking out. As they approached, they could make out frozen tins and broken crates. It was the remains of an old camp. They stopped and hopped off the sled. Celia dug around and pulled one of the tins out of the ice. It was open and empty, but stamped on the bottom was the name "S. A. Andrée" and the date "1897."

"It's like an old campsite," said Oliver. "Who was S. A. Andrée?"

"Some old explorer, I guess," said Celia. "But look!" She pointed to a narrow cut in the ice that ran up the cliff sideways like a ramp.

"See?" said Celia. "We don't have to climb after all!"

The dogs raced forward with the sled, bouncing over the uneven ground and running up the narrow cut in the ice.

"Wait up!" Oliver and Celia ran behind the sled, listening nervously to the sounds of thumping, hammering, and crashing from beneath the ice. They used the cobalt-blue walls of ice beside them to help themselves along, moving side by side. A narrow slit of blue sky was visible at the end of the ramp.

"Is it just me," Oliver panted. "Or is this ramp getting steeper?"

"You're just in bad shape," said Celia. "Maybe if you didn't eat so many cheese puffs this wouldn't be so hard. Come on. The dogs are already up at the top."

They kept climbing, one slippery step in front of the other.

"Is it just me," Oliver said, panting, a few minutes later. "Or is that slit of sky getting narrower?"

"You're just seeing things," said Celia.

"Then why are we closer together than we were before?"

Celia looked over at her brother to where their shoulders were touching. They had been an arm's length apart when they started up the ramp after the dogs.

"The ice is closing up," said Celia. "Run!"

The twins sprinted, scrambling side by side as the ice squeezed them closer and closer together. The frozen ocean was heaving their ramp upward as the walls closed in. They ran for the sky, pushing at each other so neither fell behind, and, legs burning with the strain, they dove to the surface, sliding into the snow as the path of ice sealed itself behind them and a new ridge of ice boulders rose where the two pieces smashed together with the entire force of the Arctic Ocean.

The twins lay on their backs, looking up at the panting team of dogs. After a moment, Celia sat up.

"Wow," she said.

Oliver sat up too.

In front of them, the Arctic Ocean stretched out like the surface of the moon. It was covered in ice boulders and ridges where ice floes slammed against one another, like the one they'd just escaped.

They watched one ridge growing taller in front of them as another collapsed with a thunderous roar and a black gap of water appeared a few feet wide. They heard a cracking sound all around them.

"We'd better keep moving before the landscape changes again," said Celia.

"Okay," said Oliver, brushing himself off and shaking his hands around to get the feeling back into them. "Can I, like, keep driving?" he asked.

"Go for it," she said, happy that she got to keep riding. And, if she had to admit it, happy she could keep reading too. It turned out that you could learn a lot from a book.

Oliver smiled, feeling happier than he had any right to feel under the circumstances. "Mush! Mush!" he called, and the dogs launched themselves forward once more. He leaned and pulled on the handlebars to steer them around the uneven landscape.

The sled bumped along, jostling Celia right and left, almost knocking her off every few minutes. She struggled to read the journal some more, but she was bouncing too much to focus on the words. She looked at the pictures.

She saw another drawing of the bearded man, this time doing battle with a giant dragon. The shape was a lot like the creature whose bones they'd seen back in the cave. The pliosaur.

There is no such thing as dragons, she told herself. She couldn't let Oliver see that she was worried. He hated even the smallest lizards. A dragon would really freak him out.

She flipped the page quickly. She glanced at the image of the giant tree sticking out from the ice. Could this be yggdrasil, the World Tree? What the heck was a World Tree, anyway? Looking up at the snowy landscape in all directions, she was pretty sure there couldn't be any trees here at all. It was the middle of the ocean. The solid ground beneath them was only a few feet thick, maybe less, and it was always moving. She shut the book and put it away

"Hup-hup!" Oliver called, and the dogs ran faster. He hoped they were still going the right direction.

After a few hours, the ground flattened out. The older ice was smoother. They could slide over it more easily, with fewer turns and twists, so the dogs sped up. The graceful charge of the dogsled, the ribbons of light in the twilight sky, and the strange crackling from beneath the ice made the Navel twins very sleepy.

Looking back toward the horizon, Oliver thought he saw the silhouette of a polar bear stalking them, but when he turned to look again, it was gone. Maybe he'd made it up. The cold made thinking harder, like it was freezing up their brains, which, in fact, it was.

Oliver struggled to stay awake as he steered, leaning forward on the sled to rest his legs. Celia found her eyelids getting heavier and heavier too. With every cheerful bark of the dogs or crash of a distant ice floe, she snapped them open again, but it didn't last. Her eyelids pressed down on the world.

"Mush, mush," she heard her brother call, not as loudly as before, almost a whisper, but the dogs kept moving, pressed forward by their own love of running on the open ice.

They hardly need me at all, thought Oliver, watching through heavy eyelids as the dogs found their own way around a crack in the ice, pulling the sled safely to the other side of the narrow channel of water. "Good dogs," he murmured. He leaned on the handlebars and closed his eyes. "Just for a second," he told himself. "Just to rest for second."

On the sled, Celia was already sound asleep, and Oliver soon followed. Let it never be said of the Navel twins that there is a danger too great, or a condition too perilous, that they could not sleep through it.

It was their good fortune to have a team of skillful sled dogs pulling them along who needed no more encouragement than the joy of running.

It was their bad fortune, however, to still have a polar bear on their trail.

The great beast moved slowly among the floes, stopping between boulders to sniff the air, swimming across narrow channels of water where the ice had broken, tracking them. With the scarcity of food this far north, it has been said that a hungry polar bear will sometimes track its prey for hundreds of miles across the ice.

And this bear, we should note, was very hungry.

23

WE ARE NOT BRUNCH

"YOU NEVER KNOW what you'll learn when you watch TV," said Claire Navel, as she and her husband watched the grainy black-and-white image on the security monitor. "Maybe Oliver and Celia are on to something."

Dr. Navel raised an eyebrow at her.

"At least when it's educational," she added. "Like this."

She tapped the screen as a large double-rotor cargo helicopter landed on top of the research station. They saw the doors open and Sir Edmund step out, wearing a fluffy white snowsuit with a thick fur hood and oversized goggles. His big mustache gave him a walrusy look, and Claire Navel, in spite of the danger her family was in, had to chuckle.

"I can't believe *he's* my mortal enemy," she said.

"*Our* mortal enemy," corrected Dr. Navel.

"Of course," she said, absently rubbing the spot on her finger where her ring had been. She thought of her children, racing across the ice on a dogsled, and exhaled sharply. She wouldn't let Sir Edmund and Janice get away with all they had put the twins through. They might be villainous, but their evil schemes were nothing compared to a mother's wrath. They'd get their comeuppance.

She smiled again. She really liked the word *comeuppance*.

On the screen, Sir Edmund was shouting orders at the men who had arrived with him, and they started unloading a giant crate from the back of the big helicopter. It was at least twenty feet long. It took eight large men to carry it.

Janice ran up the metal stairs to the landing pad to greet Sir Edmund, her eyes glancing briefly at the crate, snow blowing up into her face with the wind from the rotor blades. She shouted something to Sir Edmund. The Doctors Navel couldn't hear what was being said, but by the way Janice was gesturing, it looked like she was explaining how she planned to do them in. She even laughed.

Sir Edmund did not look amused.

Janice seemed disappointed and did some more explaining. Sir Edmund gestured back.

"I think they're coming this way," said Dr. Navel. "Sir Edmund wants to talk to us."

"How can you tell?" his wife asked.

"Because that's what he just said." Dr. Navel shrugged. "I learned to read lips while you were away. It passed the time."

His wife hugged him; she was impressed.

"I won't ever go away like that again," she promised. "Once Oliver and Celia are back, we'll always stick together."

Dr. Navel smiled, although part of him didn't believe it. He knew his wife was as much daredevil as parent, and sometimes the daredevil side of her won out. But he would always be there to put things back together when she returned.

"So what do we do now?" he asked. "There could be a problem when they see that the twins have escaped."

"At least it will be our problem, not Oliver and Celia's. They're safer out on the ice than in here with those two."

She changed the channel to the hallway so they could see Janice and Sir Edmund coming, with the rest of his thugs for backup.

"And it will be nice to see the look on Edmund's face when he sees they're gone," she added.

"But what if he goes after them?"

"I'm sure he'll go after them," she said. "But he'll have to get through us first."

Sir Edmund stood outside the steel door and stared up at it.

"So they're on the other side of this door, huh?" he said.

"That's right," Janice told him.

He pulled at the door and tugged at the chains. "Seems strong," he said.

"It's designed to keep polar bears out; I'm sure it will hold the Navels in."

"You're sure, are you?" Sir Edmund stroked his mustache. The Navels had escaped his clutches more times than he could count. He did not want to underestimate them again. He had his own ideas on how to keep them contained. "There's no other way out?"

"No," said Janice, starting to get offended that Sir Edmund didn't trust her.

"You're sure?"

Janice scowled at him. She did not appreciate her villainy being questioned. She had raided the tombs of the ancient kings of Burma to steal the Jade Toothpicks; she had stolen the identity of a famed Tibetan mountain climber; she had kidnapped more explorers than she could count. She could certainly keep the Navels prisoner!

"I've brought you closer to Atlantis than you've ever been, and you doubt me?" she crossed her arms.

"I suppose you're right," said Sir Edmund. "I guess I have no further need of your services."

"So that's it? I'm done?"

"You are," said Sir Edmund.

"Then I want my money."

"You will be generously paid for your work." Sir Edmund smiled. "I trust bars of gold will be acceptable to you?"

"Oh yes," she said, "they will." She tried to suppress her smile. It did not suit a grave robber to giggle like a schoolgirl.

"Good," said Sir Edmund. "I've had my men unload it into the upper cargo bay. You can get it there."

He was barely done speaking when Janice rushed up the tunnel toward the cargo bay.

"You'll need the combination to unlock it," he called after her.

"I'll pick the lock!" she called back, not breaking her stride. She wasn't about to turn around and give Sir Edmund a chance to trick her out of the gold she'd been promised. She wasn't going to do anything else until she saw the gold with her own eyes.

Once she was out of Sir Edmund's sight, she skipped down the tunnel. Her partner Frank had been fed to a yeti, her next partner, Ernest, had just been thrown in jail in Djibouti with that pirate, Bonnie. Janice was the only one left, which suited her fine. When it came to gold, she didn't like to share.

"Nice knowing you," Sir Edmund whispered, a devious little smirk spreading across his devious little face. He ran his fingers along the giant fossil in the wall. And exhaled, content.

On the other side of the door, Dr. Navel's eyes were glued to the security monitor, watching Janice and Sir Edmund talk. They were turned away from the camera so he couldn't read their lips, but he watched Janice run off. He kept having to wipe the screen off as water dripped down from the ceiling.

The whole roof of the room was sagging inward with the weight of water above it. The ice was melting, and soon the weight of the earth pressing down would cause a collapse. It was amazing the disasters that a few extra degrees of warmth could cause in the Arctic Circle.

"We had better hurry," he said.

"Just a few more minutes," said his wife, stepping up behind him. "I want to see what made Janice run off so quickly. See if you can find her."

Dr. Navel pressed a button on the remote and the screen changed to a picture of the empty kennel with the gate swinging open. He hit it again and just saw static.

"Sorry," he said. "Oliver and Celia are better at this sort of thing."

After some more fiddling they saw the helicopter already crusted with ice, and then the large cargo bay with the one long crate sitting in the middle of the floor. Janice came rushing over to it.

"Got it!" said Dr. Navel.

"What do you think is in that crate?" his wife whispered.

"I thought that's why we're watching," said Dr. Navel. "To find out."

"It was a rhetorical question," she replied. "I didn't expect you to answer."

They watched as Janice bent down and fiddled with the lock on the crate.

"She's picking the lock," said Dr. Navel.

"You don't need to narrate, honey," said Claire. "I'm watching too."

Janice stood again. She smiled and lifted the lid of the crate. From the angle, the explorers couldn't see into it, but they watched her face as the smile vanished. Her eyebrows furrowed with confusion. Then her face turned into a mask of terror. Her mouth opened wide, and even through the thick ice and the steel doors they heard her muffled scream just before something pulled her into the crate and she was gone.

"Um," was all that Dr. Navel could think to say.

They watched in horror as the large crate shook and rattled on the floor. They saw Janice's hands reach out, trying to pull herself free, but just as her head came into view again, whatever was inside the crate pulled her back in. The crate stopped shaking. The cargo bay was still.

"What was that?" said Dr. Navel, stepping away from the screen, as if the thing in the box could come through the security camera to get him. "What is in that box?"

"It could be anything," said Claire. "Sir Edmund's private zoo is filled with rare, exotic, and dangerous creatures."

"Well, I am the world's leading cryptozoologist, after all," Sir Edmund said, stepping into the room. The Navels spun around. They hadn't even heard him unlock the chains and open the door, but now he stood before them stroking his big red mustache, with two of his thugs behind him.

"You're no more than a poacher," said Dr. Navel. "You steal these creatures from their homes and put them in cages. You once set a yeti on Oliver and Celia!"

"And a kraken," added his wife.

"Oh yes, that was delightful," said Sir Edmund. "But nothing compared to what I've brought this time! It took quite some doing to capture it."

"I think I know what it is," said Claire.

"You do?" asked Sir Edmund.

"You do?" asked Dr. Navel.

"I do," she said. "And you're crazy. If that thing

gets out, it is impossible to control. It could eat you too."

"What is it?" Dr. Navel asked.

"Do you want to tell him, or should I?" Sir Edmund asked her. "I mean, I can't believe he hasn't figured it out . . . there's a fossil of one frozen in the wall on the other side of the door."

"You mean—" Dr. Navel gulped.

"Yeah," sighed Claire. "Sir Edmund just fed Janice to a dragon for lunch."

"Is it really lunchtime already?" Sir Edmund checked his watch. "I think I would say she was more like brunch."

"Dragons don't eat brunch," said Claire Navel.

"I believe I'm the expert here," said Sir Edmund. "The dragon is from my zoo, after all, and I say Janice was brunch."

"A person can't be brunch," said Claire.

"To a dragon she can," said Sir Edmund.

"You need breakfast and lunch food together for it to be brunch."

"You do not."

"At least coffee or juice."

"Dragons don't drink coffee or juice."

"Then Janice wasn't brunch."

"She was."

"She wasn't."

"She was!"

"She wasn't!" Claire Navel stomped her foot. "A dragon does not eat brunch!"

"A dragon eats whatever a dragon wants!" Sir Edmund's face got red.

Dr. Navel grabbed his wife's hand. He couldn't believe she was arguing about this. She nodded at him that it was okay. She knew what she was doing.

Sir Edmund's eyes narrowed. He knew what she was doing too. She was trying to distract him. He bent down and looked under the table. He peered behind a filing cabinet.

"Where are your brats?" he asked, then he saw the open grate to the air-conditioning vent. "No," he said, his face turning a brighter red than his facial hair. "No!"

He turned to his thugs and barked at them. "Search the station. Search the ice! Find Oliver and Celia and bring them back here! Find them now!" He looked back at their parents. "You'll regret this," he said and stormed out of the room. "Lunch, dinner, a midnight snack . . . whatever it is, I promise I will feed the lot of you to that dragon!"

"As long as it isn't brunch!" Claire Navel shouted after him defiantly as the doors slammed. They heard the chains snapping back into place. The Navels glanced nervously at each other.

Claire Navel smiled. "I bought us a little time," she said. "And now Sir Edmund's mad. No one thinks clearly when he's mad."

"You have a plan?" Dr. Navel pursed his lips.

His wife nodded.

"We're breaking out?"

She nodded again.

"What's the plan?"

"I was thinking of calling it the Polar Plot."

"Not a bad name," said Dr. Navel. "How do we do it?"

"That's the part you're not going to like so much."

Dr. Navel listened to his wife's plan and reluctantly agreed. If it worked, they would escape, find Oliver and Celia, and discover Atlantis together. If it failed, the twins would never see their parents again.

24

WE SLEEP WITH WALRUSES

IT CAME AS quite a shock to Oliver and Celia when they woke up, lurching to a stop at the edge of a wide crack in the ice at least as long as a football field. It came as even more of a shock that they were surrounded by a herd of walruses, hundreds of them, snoring and growling and trumpeting at each other in what Wally the Word Worm would call a cacophony, and the rest of us would simply call loud.

Oliver, still leaning on the handlebars, stuck to them by his frozen gloves, snapped his eyes open to find himself face to face with a large bull walrus. Its whiskers tickled his cheeks and its large tusks pointed down past his knees. It had a huge scar down the left side of its face that made it look like a grizzled veteran of long ago battles.

The walrus snorted once and Oliver fell backward off the sled and into the snow.

Celia chuckled and the scar-faced walrus turned toward her, lifting its bulky body up to tower over her. Celia, as we know, was not someone who would allow herself to be bullied by an animal, even if it weighed over a hundred times more than she did and had two hard ivory tusks threatening to impale her. She'd faced down a giant squid before. She could handle a walrus.

She pulled up her goggles, stood up as straight as she could underneath the walrus and puffed out her chest. She glared. The walrus reared back farther, its tusks hanging perilously above Celia's head.

The walrus roared.

Celia roared right back.

The walrus snorted once and turned to the side. It flopped onto its belly and moved away down the ice, grunted and growling. The other walruses, seeing that this strange little creature had stared down their leader, also moved away, clearing a nice spot on the ice for the Navel twins and their sled dogs.

Celia nodded, happy that she had established her dominance. The walrus wasn't so different than Oliver first thing in the morning.

"Well, now what?" said Oliver, looking over the herd of walruses to the ocean beyond.

The nearest ice was floating at least a hundred yards away across freezing-cold water.

"How would I know?" said Celia. "Why don't you check the compass?"

Oliver looked at his feet.

Celia's shoulders slumped. "You lost it, didn't you?" She frowned.

Oliver shrugged. "Kind of."

"How do you kind of lose it? You either lost it or you didn't!"

"I lost it."

"I knew it!"

"If you knew it," said Oliver, "then why did you give it to me in the first place?"

That one stumped Celia. Either she didn't know he'd lose it or she did know and she gave it to him anyway. She didn't want to admit to being wrong either way, so she ignored him and looked at the sky.

"We need to get across the water," she said. "That way is north."

"How do you know?"

"It's getting dark," said Celia. "And that's the North Star." She pointed at a bright spot in the sky.

"How can you tell? I can see more than one star."

"Episode 237 of *Love at 30,000 Feet*," said Celia. "Captain Sinclair falls in love with an astronomer who turns out to be a figment of his imagination, but she tells him how to navigate by the finding the star just off the end of the Little Dipper constellation. It's always right above the North Pole. And that's where we need to go."

"Okay," said Oliver. "But it's getting dark."

"I just said that," said Celia.

"I mean, I think we should camp here."

Celia nodded. She was tired too. Exhausted, really, and cold and could use a good night's sleep. Or at least as good a night's sleep as she could have sharing a tent with her brother on an Arctic ice sheet surrounded by a herd of walruses.

Oliver started pulling supplies off the sled. The dogs looked at him eagerly.

"I think they want to eat," said Celia.

"So do I," said Oliver, rummaging. He pulled out another bag of cheese puffs and started eating it. The dogs wagged their tails and whimpered.

"You aren't going to share?" said Celia.

"Dogs eat dog food," he said.

"You eat like a walrus," said Celia. "Too bad we don't have any walrus food."

Oliver smiled and held two long, curled cheese puffs so they hung out of his mouth like walrus tusks. He roared at Celia. She put her arms on her sides and gave him a look that would have frozen the ocean, if it weren't already frozen.

Oliver stopped roaring. Celia shook her head and pulled out a bag of dry dog food that was underneath the case of cheese puffs. She dumped it onto the snow. As the dogs dug in to their kibble, Oliver went back to the sled to find a tent and start setting it up.

Celia stared out at the cold ocean, thinking her hardest about how to get across, but no ideas were coming to her.

"You could help me out, you know?" Oliver called back to her, struggling to keep the wind from blowing the tent over before he could get the poles in. Every time he got one corner up, the other would blow down.

"I'm trying to figure out what we're supposed to do," said Celia. "We don't have a boat."

"Sleep," said Oliver.

"I don't suppose there are toothbrushes or pajamas on that sled?" Celia wondered.

"I don't think the walruses care if we brush

our teeth," said Oliver. "And it's too cold to change into pajamas anyway. I'm sleeping in everything I have on."

Celia guessed her brother was right and she helped him finish setting up the tent. The dogs were already curled into a pile, snoozing happily in the snow. Their paws twitched and they made high-pitched whimpers as they dreamed about chasing squirrels or walruses or whatever it was sled dogs dreamed about. She crawled inside with Oliver and they snuggled into two slippery sleeping bags, zipped up so just their faces stuck out.

With all the honking and snorting from the walruses, Celia wondered how they'd ever get any sleep at all, then she realized that Oliver was already as sound asleep as the dogs outside. Celia was amazed how similar her brother could be to a drooling Siberian husky.

"Figures," she grumbled.

She couldn't sleep. She unzipped her bag again and sat up with a flashlight, shivering and reading the old leather explorer's journal. His handwriting grew messier toward the end.

Nearly arrived. Journey much harder than I imag-

ined. Ran out of food. The dogs are starving, but I need them to pull the sled. Forced to make soup from my boot leather and share it with them.

"Gross," Celia grunted.

Frostbite on my toes now. A polar bear stalked me for days, but this morning I reached a most remarkable place. A frozen canyon opened before my eyes, all ice and crimson snow. What should make the snow turn red, I do not know. I have had frightening dreams each night, visions perhaps, of Ratatosk, the gossiping squirrel, warning me to turn back. But I cannot turn back. I must press onward through the canyon, over the bones of ancient giants, to the lost city of the north. Only there will the library be safe. I hear a roar in the distance. Perhaps the bear has followed again, driven mad with hunger. Or perhaps the stories are true . . . perhaps here there be dragons. The days to come will tell.

There were no more entries after that until the last one, that he'd written thousands of miles away, hiding in a cavern on a desert island. Whatever happened in between, he didn't write about. He probably went mad, dreaming about squirrels who gossiped and dragons who roared.

Listening to the cacophony outside, Celia almost thought she heard the roar of a dragon in the wind. And the chattering of the walruses sure did sound like the other kids in sixth grade gossiping.

Thinking about sixth grade made Celia homesick. Not just for the TV, but for their apartment at the Explorers Club, and for their mother and father, together at home after all this time, and for boring stuff like eating vegetables, doing homework, and even climbing the rope in gym class.

She felt her eyelids growing heavy again, felt herself finally drifting to sleep to the gentle sounds of the ice cracking and shifting, and the water lapping up against the edge of the ice, and the cold quiet of the Arctic lulling her to sleep.

Her eyes snapped wide open again.

The cold quiet.

But it wasn't supposed to be quiet. How long had she been asleep?

"Oliver!" she poked at her brother. "Oliver wake up! Oliver!"

Oliver opened one eye and scowled. "I'm tired," he said.

"Listen," said Celia. "You hear that?"

"What?" said Oliver, propping himself up on his arms. "I don't hear anything."

"Exactly!" said Celia. "What happened to the walruses? And why aren't the dogs snoring anymore?"

"Oh," said Oliver, sitting up all the way.

"Oh is right," said Celia. "Go look outside."

"Me?" said Oliver. "Why me? Why do I always have to—"

Celia raised her eyebrows at him.

"Right," he said. "My catchphrase."

He slithered out of his sleeping bag and put his hood up and went to the edge of the tent. He peeked out.

"There's no more walruses," said Oliver.

Celia started to bundle herself up to see.

"The dogs are gone too," he said.

"What!" Celia pulled herself up behind her brother. "Where'd they go?"

"They didn't go anywhere," said Oliver, and he opened the tent flap wider. "We did."

Celia stuck her head outside and gasped. Their tent was in the middle of a small circle of ice floating away from the shore, where the herd of walruses slept soundly.

"We broke off!" Celia cried out. "We're adrift!"

25

WE'RE DRIFTERS

"WE'RE FLOATING INTO the Arctic Ocean," Oliver declared.

In the distance, the dogs stood beside the sled on the edge of the mainland, barking as their masters floated away on an island of ice.

Celia's shoulders sagged.

She should have known.

For her and her brother, it was pretty certain that whenever something could go wrong, it would.

On shore, she saw the dogs looking around at the walruses and at each other and then, lastly, at a polar bear as it came charging through the snow.

Huskies are very loyal dogs and very intelligent too. At this point, their little dog brains must have been struggling between their loyalty and their intelligence. Loyalty told them to stay and look after their masters. Intelligence told them that six dogs were no match for a hungry polar bear. Intelligence, it seemed, won out. They took off together hauling the sled behind, barking and racing back in the direction from which they'd come.

The polar bear ignored the dogs, rushing instead into the middle of the herd of walruses. Most of the walruses dove into the water to escape, but some of the bigger ones turned to fight. Oliver and Celia had seen enough nature programs to know what gruesome scene would come next.

They turned away. Hearing the roars and growls of bear-on-walrus combat was enough for them, they didn't need to see it too.

Fleeing walruses raced beneath the surface to the ice field on the opposite shore. Some of the walruses came by the little chunk of ice on which the twins were floating, bumping it and making it tilt and shudder in the water. Some of them tore chunks off as they rushed by, knocking holes and watery cracks into it.

"Watch it!" Oliver yelled, as if the panicked walruses could understand.

Another bumped into the ice floe, and another.

Oliver lost his footing and fell again. Celia grabbed him and pulled him to the center, where the ice was the most stable. They looked to the distant field of ice, the path to the North Pole, where the walruses were leaping back onto the ice with a great flurry of roars and honks. The twins were drifting away from it.

Instead of going toward the ice, they were being pushed out to sea. With just their tent and a few bags of cheese puffs that Oliver had brought in for a late-night snack, they didn't have enough supplies to last very long.

"If we don't get across to that ice," said Oliver, "we'll never survive on the ocean."

"Duh," said Celia.

She tried to come up with an idea. Random thoughts raced through her head, about Djibouti and dragons, Janice and squirrels, the theme song from *The World's Best Rodeo Clown*. For those of us who have ever had to come up with an idea, we know how annoying it can be when other thoughts keep popping up to distract us.

"Think, Celia!" she told herself. They were getting farther and farther into the open water. "Stop thinking about rodeo clowns!"

"That's it!" said Oliver. "You did it!"

"What?" said Celia. "What did I do?"

"Rodeo clowns!" Oliver cheered and started taking apart their tent.

"Huh?" Celia wondered. It wasn't usual for her to be the puzzled one.

"Help me get the tent apart," said Oliver. "Quickly."

Celia hesitated.

"Come on!" Oliver yelled. "We don't want to miss our chance! We need to rope a walrus!"

"We need to *what*?"

"It was your idea!" said Oliver. "We're gonna snag a walrus with this tent. He'll drag us to shore."

Celia looked at the water. Only a few walruses were racing below. If they didn't do it now, they'd miss their chance. She rushed over and helped Oliver with the tent.

"Okay," he said. "When a walrus passes under, we'll drop it over the side and it'll swim right into the tent like a net. Then it'll drag us to shore."

"What if the tent breaks?" Celia wondered.

"It won't," said Oliver.

"How do you know?"

"Because you made me watch *Celebrity Fashion Crimes*," said Oliver.

Celia remembered what Madam Mumu said about her tent dress. Warm, fireproof . . . and indestructible.

"On three," said Oliver as two walruses raced toward them just below the surface of the water. "One . . . two . . . three!"

They tossed the tent into the water. The walruses hit it as they came out from underneath. Oliver and Celia leaned back and dug their heels into the ice. The large sea mammals were too big and moving too fast. They dragged the twins across the top of their floating island. The back side pulled up into the air as the walruses surged forward; the front edge plowed into the water and tipped them forward.

"Oops!" Oliver shouted, just before he and his sister slid off the end.

As the ice-cold water hit him like a punch in the face and the walruses pulled him below the surface, he realized that he probably should have thought the plan through a little harder.

Just before she went under, Celia remembered why she was the one who usually came up with the plans.

26

WE FIGHT FOR OUR LIVES

CELIA TURNED HER head to the side, still holding the tent in both her fists, and holding her breath with just as much effort. She opened her eyes and saw the blurry shape of her brother stilling clinging to his strip of the tent. She was glad he hadn't let go either. If they made it out of the water, she wanted the chance to yell at him.

Of course, she figured, they'd probably freeze to death seconds later.

She could tell by the pull against her heavy clothes that they were moving very fast. The walruses were in a panic now and plunging forward blindly, making loud bell-like noises. You would probably panic too if you were fleeing from a polar bear and suddenly some kids dropped a tent over your head. You probably would not make loud bell-like noises, as you do not have a walrus's air-filled throat sac to make them with, which is also why you couldn't hold your breath very long. Oliver and Celia were just realizing that now.

The cold water began to feel like a thousand tiny needles poking into their skin. Celia couldn't feel her toes or her fingers. Oliver wasn't certain he still had a nose.

Suddenly, they broke the surface, bursting into the light and the air. The walruses crashed up onto the ice sheet, sliding forward and dragging the twins behind. They let go of the tent and rolled onto their sides as the two creatures bucked and bellowed underneath the fabric.

"They looked like they're playing ghosts . . ." Oliver panted. "Except . . . they don't have . . . eye holes."

"You . . ." Celia panted. Her whole body started to shiver. ". . . almost drowned us."

"We . . . made it . . . didn't we?"

Celia looked around. "No," she said.

They hadn't made it across the water to the other side. They were back on the ice sheet where they had started. They were no closer to the North Pole than before, except now they were wet and had no dogs and no supplies. They saw the tracks of the dogsled leading away through the snow.

"The walruses must have turned around while we were underwater," said Oliver. "They couldn't see through the sheet."

"Wait," said Celia. "That means the bear is here too!" She turned and saw the polar bear battling the scar-faced walrus closer to her than she liked to be to the front of the classroom in school. She jumped backward, pulling her brother with her.

The two walruses the twins had ridden shook off the tent and rushed forward to help their fellow walrus. When three walruses fight a polar bear, the sound is something like an angry mob in Djibouti, except with more bone-crunching noises.

"I think we'd better get out of here," Celia suggested.

"We still need to get across the ice somehow," said Oliver.

"We'll freeze to death if we don't get somewhere warm and dry. Have you ever heard of hypothermia?"

"Duh," said Oliver. "It's when your body temperature gets below 95 degrees and you can't get warm and your organs stop working and you freeze to death. I told you I watch as much educational programming as you do and I'm tired of you thinking I'm dumb."

"I don't think you're dumb!" said Celia.

"You always act like you do."

"You're my brother; that's how I have to act."

"Who says?"

"Everyone!" said Celia. "That's how sisters treat their little brothers!"

"I'm not your little brother! You're only older by three minutes!"

"And forty-two seconds," said Celia. "*You* always leave that out."

"Because it doesn't matter! We're the same age!"

"You're my little brother!"

"I am not!"

"You are!"

As they argued, the battle between bear and walrus raged behind them. Flesh was torn, teeth gnashed, and the ice was stained with blood, yet the fight continued. Every time the bear swung his claws at one walrus, another would swing his entire body into the bear from his exposed side.

Thousands of pounds of fat and muscle crashed into each other. Oliver and Celia hardly noticed.

"Well, I'm not dumb!" Oliver yelled.

"I never said you were!"

"You always say I am and you never say you're sorry!"

"I'm sorry that *you* think that *I* think that *you're* dumb!" said Celia.

"That's not an apology!" said Oliver.

"Well, I have nothing to be sorry about! I didn't come up with the plan that gave us hypothermia!"

"At least I had a plan!"

"I have a plan too!"

"Oh yeah? What's that?"

"To keep yelling at you! Because yelling at you is keeping me warm!"

"Me too!" yelled Oliver.

"So we need to keep fighting or we'll freeze to death!"

"But now I'm not angry at you anymore!"

"What if I called you dumb again?" she yelled.

"It's not the same if you don't mean it." Oliver stopped yelling. He shivered.

"What if I do mean it?" Celia yelled, getting right in his face.

"You're my sister," said Oliver. "I know that you don't really mean it."

He didn't feel angry anymore. Actually, he didn't feel anything anymore. Just tired. Had he been thinking more clearly, he would have known that being suddenly sleepy and not caring about things like freezing to death or bear-and-walrus battles going on behind you were symptoms of hypothermia.

Celia glanced over his shoulder at the bear-and-walrus fight. It looked like they had reached a standoff. The bear was circling the walruses, and the walruses were huddled together, growling and snorting at the bear. Neither side had the strength for another attack, but neither side wanted to retreat.

Celia felt the same way. She was tired, but she knew that fighting was the only way to keep both of them warm, so she was not going to retreat. If they stopped arguing, their body temperature would go down even more. Oliver might already have hypothermia, so she had to yell at him again, she had to get him mad. She thought of the one thing that would insult him more than anything else.

"I bet you're not mad because you like exploring!" Celia accused him. "You're just like Mom and Dad!"

Oliver shrugged. He wasn't mad. In fact, it was kind of true. The walrus-and-bear battle was pretty cool. He'd never seen anything like it on TV. And he liked driving the dogsled too.

"Maybe you're right," he said.

"No!" Celia yelled. "I'm not right! You need to be mad! You're Oliver Navel, my brother, and you hate exploring and you hate when I'm right and you want to argue with me because I always make you go first and act like you're dumb!"

"But I don't want to argue anymore," said Oliver. He thought if he could just sleep for a minute, maybe he'd be ready to argue when he woke up. He closed his eyes.

"Hey!" Celia snapped in his face. "You need to stay awake! Focus! Get angry!"

"Can'tgetangryatmysister," mumbled Oliver. He started to sway on his feet. He felt silly. He felt confused. He couldn't talk straight. "Sister," he repeated. "You're my best friend."

"You're mine too, Oliver," said Celia. If Oliver was in his right mind he never would have said that to her face and she would never have said it back to him, but times were desperate. She had to do something drastic. She slapped him across the face and yelled, "Wake up!" She slapped him again.

He smiled dumbly, half opening his eyes. He wasn't even shivering anymore.

"Don't close your eyes!" Celia yelled.

Hearing the noise of Celia's yelling, the polar bear turned its head and looked toward her. It sniffed the air. The walruses bellowed and puffed their chests. That was all the encouragement the polar bear needed to go after easier prey. The two human children wouldn't give him as much meat as a walrus, not by a long shot, but they'd be as easy to eat as cheese puffs.

He turned and began to stalk toward them.

Celia saw the bear coming over her shoulder. It was moving slowly, tired from its fight. Its mouth was ringed red with walrus blood; chunks of torn blubber clung to its claws. Its dark eyes showed no emotion, like the twins' eyes after five hours of Saturday morning cartoons.

The walruses, all three of them exhausted and perhaps still angry for the tent trick that Oliver had tried to pull on them, immediately dove into the water and swam for the far shore of the ice field. They weren't about to risk their lives to save two human children. They had their own walrus families to worry about. Before he dove, the scar-faced one may have even waved a mocking flipper at Celia.

"Jerk walrus," Celia grumbled. "Oliver," she turned back to her brother. "You have to wake up . . . we have to run. The bear's coming . . ."

"I'm just gonna take a quick nap." Oliver sighed, flopping down in the snow. "You can wake me when the show's over."

"You're not making sense," said Celia. "We're not watching TV. A polar bear is really coming to eat us."

"Offer it some cheese puffs." Oliver laid down in the snow. It made perfect sense to him. Why would a polar bear want to eat him when cheese puffs have that extra-cheesy crunch?

"No!" Celia begged. "Come on! Please!" She grabbed Oliver's arm and pulled, trying to lift him. She couldn't, so she started to drag him through the snow, struggling backward while facing the bear. It lowered its head and kept creeping forward, its cruel eyes fixed on her. "Shoo, bear!" Celia shouted. "Shoo!"

The bear did not shoo. It rushed toward her. She reached into her pocket and pulled out the canister of bear repellent, pointing it at the bear, turning her ahead away, and squinting back as she sprayed. The bear ran right into the mist and stopped. It shook its head. It blinked.

"Yeah!" said Celia, sniffing the air. It smelled peppery. "Stay back!"

As she dragged Oliver away, the bear stepped forward with every step she took backward. Celia stepped and the bear stepped. Celia stopped and the bear stopped. Every time it got too close she raised the bear spray and gave him a spritz. The bear backed off and growled, low and threatening. Celia knew then that if she turned her back or if she fell or if—no, when—she ran out of bear repellent, both she and her brother would meet a most gruesome end.

She had to keep moving.

The fate of the Navels was in her very cold, shaking hands.

27

WE BEAR THE UNBEARABLE

ICE HAD FORMED all over her clothes and over her hair and along her cheeks. Luckily, her clothes were dry underneath the cold-weather gear. The duct tape had kept the water out. That was probably the only reason she and her brother hadn't frozen to death yet.

She took another careful step backward.

The bear took another step forward.

"Come on, Oliver," she groaned, pulling him.

"Just leave me," he mumbled, half awake.

"I'm not leaving my little brother," she answered.

"We're the same age," he replied, opening his eyes.

"Are not!" Celia pulled.

"Are too!" Oliver kicked his feet a little, pushing himself up as she pulled. He had some life in him yet.

Unfortunately, Celia had not actually expected her brother to push himself up, and so when he pushed, she pulled too hard and they both fell down. The bear repellent fell out of Celia's hand.

The polar bear charged.

It bounded across the snow at them, and reared up to pin them both beneath its paws. Out of instinct Celia dove to protect her little brother, although Oliver dove at the same moment to protect Celia—who was, after all, only older by three minutes and forty-two seconds—and they smacked heads right into each other and bounced back in opposite directions.

The bear's paw came down in between them, smashing harmlessly into the snow. It turned to bite at Oliver, who kicked it in the snout, and then it spun to snap at Celia, who punched it in the same spot, and then it stood to its full height again. It roared.

The twins scrambled backward. The bear hesitated, looking from twin to twin, but it didn't attack.

"What's it doing?" Oliver yelled across to his sister on the other side of the bear.

"I think my punch stunned it!" she said.

"I think my kick stunned it," said Oliver.

"I think it's deciding which of us is tastier!" said Celia. "Run!"

Oliver pushed himself up and ran. Celia grabbed the canister off the ground and sprayed it. It fizzled, empty. She threw it at the bear and ran after her brother.

They sprinted, slipping and sliding on the ice. The bear hesitated, unsure how much energy it could waste on a stringy child. It sniffed at the empty canister. When the twins met up about a half a football field's length away, the bear started toward them again at a trot. Time was on its side.

"We can't slow down." Celia panted. Her sweat had already frozen against her skin underneath her clothes. She felt herself shivering uncontrollably. "The bear is just waiting for us to slow down."

Side by side, the twins helped each other along, stumbling through the snow. The bear followed, never taking its eyes off of them.

"I feel tired again," said Oliver.

"Me too," said Celia.

"I can't feel my feet," he added.

"Me neither," said Celia.

They trudged on, the minutes passed. Or

maybe it was hours. They couldn't know how long they'd been walking. The light never changed. The aurora borealis still waved above them. Neither of them spoke. It was too hard to speak. Celia wanted to argue to keep them warm, but she didn't have the strength. The cold was shutting her body down. Oliver had started mumbling again, talking about *Bizarro Bandits* and *Rodeo Clowns*.

"Do you think they have cable TV in Atlantis?" he mumbled. "I hope they do. I'd like to see Corey Brandt again, even if it's just on *Sunset High*. I'm glad he ended up with Lauren on that show. She seemed nice."

Celia didn't answer him. She didn't even have the energy to argue for Team Annabel or to talk about Corey Brandt or television or anything. She was too cold and too tired and too afraid of being eaten by a polar bear.

As she trudged along, she didn't hear her brother behind her anymore. She worried she would have to drag him again because his brain had frozen or something. She turned and saw Oliver standing still in the snow.

The bear in the distance stopped too and watched them. He waited for one of them to fall.

For a bear, a frozen child on the ground was just like a Popsicle. Celia did not want to become a Popsicle.

"Oliver, we can't stop here," she said. "Keep going."

"I think we should climb," he said.

"What?" Celia clomped over to him through the snow. "Did your brain freeze?"

"I think he wants us to climb?" Oliver repeated.

"What are you talking about? Who wants us to climb?"

"Him." Oliver pointed up. High in the air above them floated a shining silver ball with a basket hanging below it. A rope dropped down from the basket.

Just then, a bearded man wearing big goggles and a brown parka leaned over the edge of the basket.

"Quickly!" he yelled. "Climb up here!"

The bear, sensing his meal might get away, charged across the ice.

"That guy looks just like Santa Claus!" Oliver smiled. "Did you see that?"

"This is a little too convenient, don't you

think?" said Celia. "I mean, haven't you heard of *deus ex machina*?"

"No," said Oliver, grabbing the rope. "But I have heard of Santa Claus."

"There's no such thing as—" Celia looked back at the bear charging toward them. "Oh, whatever."

She grabbed the rope beside her brother and the balloon lifted into the air.

The bear leaped and swiped, his steak-knife-sized claws brushing the bottom of Celia's boots, but he landed on the ice again with a crash, breaking through and smashing into the cold water.

As the twins rose away, the bear climbed out and roared, shaking the ice from its fur and trudging on the ground after them.

28

WE MEET THE ODD

WHEN THEY REACHED the basket at the top of the rope, the man pulled them in. The twins sat on the floor, out of breath, but glad to be warmed by the electric heater sitting in front of them.

They looked up at the man, trying to figure out who it was who had just rescued them. His long white hair fell down over half his face and one bright blue eye gazed at the twins with a mischievous twinkle. He smiled, his bright red nose bursting like a flame from his icy white beard. He wore a light animal skin parka with a fur hood and big fuzzy white fur pants.

"Polar bear," he said, dancing from foot to foot. "You like 'em?"

"Um," said Celia.

"Oh, I know." The man shook his head. "Kids these days think wearing fur is cruel, but I'll tell you, up here, nothing goes to waste. Meat, bone, blood, and fur. You've got to use it all. A sign of respect. That bear down there would do the same to you."

"Um," said Oliver.

"The parka is reindeer skin," he added.

Oliver shuddered. "Santa?" he asked, dreading the idea of Father Christmas wearing his reindeer as a jacket.

The man laughed a jolly laugh, pulled off his glove, and stuck out his big red palm at Oliver. "Odd."

He frowned at the man and crossed his arms in front of himself. "I am not."

"No! Of course not." The man laughed. "But I am! Odd. Odd's my name!"

"Odd?" said Celia. "Your name is Odd?"

"Odd is not a good name?" the man smirked.

"No," said Celia. "It's . . . it's just . . . you know . . . odd."

"Exactly!" Odd laughed. "And it's quite a common name in these parts. Be right back!"

He turned and started pulling on ropes and levers, which unwound springs, which turned pedals, which spun rotor blades on the back of the basket, steering it over the open water, across the craggy ice, above the honking herd of walruses, and toward the horizon. Two dark ravens swooped and flapped around the balloon, cawing as they flew.

"I told you he wasn't Santa Claus," whispered Celia.

"You said he was a *deus ex machina*," Oliver answered her. "He doesn't look like it to me."

"No one looks like it," said Celia. "*Deus ex machina* is a plot device."

"You think he's plotting something?"

"No!" Celia rolled her eyes. "It's a storytelling trick. Something helpful that appears just when all hope seems lost and fixes all the main characters' problems."

"You think he's going to fix all our problems?" Oliver sat up straight, hopeful.

"No," said Celia. "I think he's going to make a lot more problems."

"How do you know?"

"He looks like the man in the drawings," she said. "That means he'll probably be all mysterious and we'll end up getting chased across the ice by a monster or something. That's how these stories go."

"What stories?"

"Ours," said Celia.

The man came back over to them.

"Well, as I was saying, I am Odd. Very glad I found you. That bear looked mighty determined."

"Yeah, thanks for being our *deus ex mechanic*," said Oliver.

"*Machina*," said Celia. "Sorry, my brother doesn't pay attention to educational programming."

"I do too," Oliver grumbled.

"My name's Celia and this is—" Celia began, but the man interrupted her.

"Oliver," said Odd.

"What?" Oliver's jaw dropped. "How did you know that? Are you . . . a shaman?"

"Of course he's a shaman," said Celia, looking at the man's long beard and one piercing blue eye.

Celia and Oliver had met shamans all over the world, people who could speak with the spirits and know things that no one else could know. Every society had shamans, but some listened to them more than others. In desert tribes of North Africa, shamans were tellers of stories and keepers of the culture. In the Amazon Rainforest, they were sometimes healers. Where Oliver and Celia lived, shamans were mostly people with their own talk shows.

"I bet now is when he tells us something crazy, like," she lowered her voice to an ancient groan, *"I've been expecting you . . ."*

The man smiled and lowered his hood, brushing aside the long hair that covered his other eye, revealing an eye patch embroidered with the symbol of a key in golden thread, a symbol just like the one on the golden ring in Celia's pocket and on the compass that Oliver dropped: the symbol of the Mnemones.

"Oliver and Celia Navel," said Odd, crossing his arms and leaning back on the edge of the basket, nothing but sky and two ravens circling behind him. "I'm guessing that if you're here all alone, then your mom's in trouble?"

The twins nodded.

"And you all need to get to the North Pole, because that's where Atlantis is supposed to be?"

The twins nodded again.

"And yes, Celia," Odd lowered his voice, "I have been expecting you."

29

WE DETEST DESTINY

ODD WAS NOT a shaman, at least, not professionally.

He did, however, use ancient methods for sending and receiving messages, practicing his obscure art in the solitude of the frozen north. He read symbols few others could read, and followed paths few others could follow.

"I'm a mailman," he declared proudly, pointing to the corner of the basket at three sacks, each overflowing with letters and postcards. "The only one in the Arctic Circle."

"Just a mailman?" Oliver asked, sipping the hot chocolate Odd had poured for them from a thermos.

"Just a mailman!" Odd threw his hands in the air. "It is the noblest profession!"

"I mean . . . uh . . ." Oliver didn't want to be rude. Odd's heater and his blankets and his hot chocolate and his balloon had saved them from freezing to death and being eaten by a polar bear. He was just disappointed. He'd really thought that maybe they'd been rescued by Santa Claus. That would have showed Celia.

"What my brother means, sir, is why would our mom's secret society have a mailman in it?" Celia tried more politely.

"Your mother's secret society?" Odd raised the eyebrow of his one good eye.

"Well, yeah," said Celia. "The Mnemones, the symbol on your eye patch; they were the scribes of the Lost Library and our mom's the leader."

"Did she tell you that?" Odd smirked.

Celia didn't like the tone of his voice. "No," she said. "But we heard a prophecy . . ."

Odd burst into a fit of laughter. He slapped his knee and doubled over like someone had just said Djibouti to him ten times. His nose and cheeks turned an even brighter red and he hugged himself in hysterics.

"So Mom's not the leader?" Celia tried. She did not like to be laughed at, not by her brother when she said Djibouti and not by this mailman in a balloon.

"The Mnemones are far older than the library at Alexandria," said Odd. "They are older than you can possibly imagine."

"I can imagine a lot," Celia told him.

"They are the memory keepers," said Odd.

"We know," said Celia. "We've known that for a long time now."

"But did you know that all societies have them? The scribes and storytellers, the scholars and librarians. The explorers. The mailmen."

Celia coughed.

"Excuse me," said Odd. "Mailpersons."

"Really, though? The mailmen?" Oliver didn't quite believe it.

Celia snorted at him.

"I mean, mailpersons?"

"Messengers," said Odd. "Without messengers, where would we be? Who would brave hungry polar bears and blinding snows to carry news to the far places? Who else would carry messages between the winds and the sky and the walruses?"

"Walruses don't get mail," interrupted Oliver.

"Shows what you know." Odd harrumphed.

Even though the mailman wasn't a shaman,

he sure talked as strangely as one, Oliver thought.

"Whatever," said Celia. She didn't like being told she was wrong and she didn't really need to unravel the mystery of the Mnemones. She just needed to find Atlantis, make sure the Lost Library was there, and trade Sir Edmund for it. With that done, they could go home and never do anything exciting again. She didn't really believe Sir Edmund could use a library to rule the world anyway.

"Are you taking us to the North Pole now?" she asked, unable to find the North Star in the daylight.

"I am," said Odd.

"Good," said Celia. After all they'd been through, Celia had decided not to trust anyone but her own eyes and her brother. She certainly didn't trust this mysterious one-eyed stranger in a hydrogen balloon.

"Do you know where we need to go when we get there?" Oliver asked.

Odd stroked his beard. "The ancient Norse people believe that the All-Father left the city of Asgard to hang from Yggdrasil, the World Tree, for nine days," Odd responded. "From there he could see the all the worlds below."

"Okay . . . " said Oliver, puzzled. He turned to his sister. "Why does everyone have to be so enigmatic?"

"Just because you know the word *enigmatic* doesn't mean you have to use it all the time," said Celia. "Anyway, he's talking about the North Pole. Like Dad said, when you're at the North Pole, everywhere you look is south. The entire world is *below* you."

Odd nodded slowly. "From there he could see the all the worlds below," he repeated.

"I knew that," said Oliver. He scratched an itch on his cheek. "But, uh, just to be sure . . . explain it one more time?"

"He means this World Tree thing is at the North Pole," said Celia. "If we find it, we'll find the way to Asgard."

"Okay . . . " said Oliver.

"And that's the same as Atlantis," said Celia. She thought Oliver had understood that by now.

"So we're looking for a tree?" said Oliver.

"We're looking for a tree," Celia confirmed.

"Because some dude hung from it for nine days?" said Oliver.

Celia nodded.

"So we're not looking for Santa Claus anymore?"

"They're the same," said Celia.

"All lost places are the same lost places," Odd said. *"As all lost souls are the same lost souls."*

"That's what the explorer wrote in his journal!" said Celia. "It's kind of—"

"Enigmatic," said Oliver.

Celia frowned at her brother. But he was right.

"The world is a library of stories," said Odd. "Each different, but each the same."

"Are you sure you're not a shaman?" Oliver asked.

"You will understand," said Odd, "in time."

"I really hope not," said Celia, looking over the shifting ice to the round horizon at the top of the world. She did not want to get back to sixth grade talking like a fortune cookie. She just wanted to get back to sixth grade. And save her parents. And watch TV.

Odd brought out some dinner for them in plastic containers and then returned to steering the balloon, pulling ropes and turning levers, almost as if he were following the ravens through the sky.

Oliver leaned on the basket beside Celia, watching the endless white landscape below and picking at the strange jellied meat, which oozed red and green.

"What is this?" he whispered.

"Pickled walrus liver!" Odd called back. "In lingonberry sauce! Served on a bed of seaweed."

Celia gagged.

Oliver sniffed, shrugged, and took a bite.

"Not bad, actually," he said, talking with his mouth full. Celia held her nose and ate. She didn't share her brother's appetite for Nordic cuisine. After eating they watched the ice drift below. Hours passed.

"This is boring," Oliver muttered.

"Wasn't skydiving, dogsledding, walrus roping, and escaping a polar bear enough excitement for you?" said Celia.

"I guess," said Oliver. "It's just that I don't like all this waiting around."

"You could read," Celia suggested, handing Oliver the old explorer's journal. He wrinkled his nose as he took it from her.

"Don't worry, children," said Odd. "The wait

is almost over. By morning we'll be at the pole and you'll be on your way."

"*We'll* be on our way?" Celia spun around to face him. "What do you mean? You aren't coming with us?"

"I have mail to deliver," he said.

"You're kidding," said Oliver.

"Do I look like I'm kidding?" said Odd.

He didn't.

"You have your own destiny to fulfill," he added. "I'm just an old man whose destiny is done."

"Ugh, destiny," mumbled Oliver.

"But we're just kids," said Celia.

"Kids have destinies," said Odd. "How else do they become adults?"

"Yeah," said Celia. "But most kids' destinies are about, like, the soccer team and graduation and making a macaroni picture frame."

"Not in that order," said Oliver.

"Right," said Celia. "Why is our destiny so . . ."

"Exciting?" said Oliver.

Celia scowled at him.

"Dangerous," she said. "Why does our destiny have to involve lost cities and ancient prophecies and dragons?"

"Wait, what?" said Oliver. "Dragons?"

"Growing up is far more dangerous than dragons," said Odd. "You will see."

"Wait, what about the dragons?" said Oliver. "Like, real live dragons?"

Neither Odd nor Celia was listening to him.

"Maybe I don't want to see!" Celia told Odd. "Maybe I don't want to battle dragons or discover anything! Maybe I just want my life to be normal."

"Little girl, I am sorry," said Odd. "But you don't get a choice about any of that. No one's life is normal."

"Will someone tell me about the dragons, please!" said Oliver.

"But it's not fair!" said Celia.

"That is the oldest catchphrase in the world," said Odd.

Oliver opened the journal and flipped through the pages frantically.

"It's not a catchphrase," said Celia. "It's true. Nothing is ever fair for us!"

"What do you want me to do about it?" said Odd.

"You're an adult!" yelled Celia. "Why don't you help us find this city and save our parents and protect us from all this dangerous stuff, like adults are supposed to do?"

"Aha!" said Oliver, finding the page he wanted.

"No adult can protect you from your destiny!" Odd told Celia. "Otherwise, it wouldn't be *your* destiny, it'd be theirs!"

"Well, maybe I don't want a destiny!" Celia yelled.

"Well, maybe that's too bad, because you've got one!" Odd yelled back.

"Okay, I see the dragon here," said Oliver, studying the drawing of a dragon that the explorer had put in his journal. It looked a lot like the fossilized one back in the tunnel at the research station, except this one was covered in blue-black skin and scales and had giant fearsome eyes and huge fangs. Its long body was coiled around the base of a giant tree. "Is this, like, for real?"

"Are Sir Edmund and Janice part of my destiny?" said Celia. "Because they're the ones who are going to get the Lost Library. Is it my destiny to help the bad guys win?"

"Your destiny will reveal itself to only you," said Odd.

"That's such a cop-out," said Celia.

"Celia," said Oliver, looking up from the journal.

"I knew you'd be like every other adult we've met on this search," said Celia. "You'd say a lot of strange stuff and be all enigmatic and then—"

"Celia?" said Oliver again.

"Yes, I know, that's your new favorite word," Celia snapped without looking over at her brother. Her eyes were fixed angrily on Odd. "Enigmatic," she repeated. "And then, when it came time for you to answer some real questions or offer any real help, you'd be totally unhelpful and you'd leave us in some wilderness or something. For all we know, you're lying about everything and you really work with Sir Edmund."

"Is that what you think?" said Odd.

"Celia!" Oliver shouted. She turned to him. "We're here."

Oliver pointed ahead of them to a place where the ice had split open in a wide crack, pushing against the other pieces of ice around it so there was a high wall around the opening. The snow covering the ice was veined pink and red, like it was alive.

"Crimson snow," Celia whispered. "Just like in the journal."

"Is it cursed?" Oliver shuddered.

"Algae," said Odd. "Blooms of bacteria and algae freeze in the ice and make the snow different colors."

"Good," said Oliver. He preferred the scientific answer to the mystical one. He hoped all this talk of dragons would have a similarly dull explanation.

As they flew over the wall of blue and pink and red ice and peered down into the large crack, they saw that it was not filled with the dark water of the Arctic Ocean like every other opening in the ice, but instead there was a deep canyon, at least ten stories high, and in the center, a tree, the biggest tree the twins had ever seen, poking up through a hole at the bottom, like fireman's pole in a firehouse. Its trunk disappeared into the darkness below where the ocean should have been churning. The twins would not want to slide down there.

"That's impossible," gasped Celia.

"It would be best for you to forget that phrase," said Odd, as he steered the balloon down between the narrow walls of ice. The canyon creaked and groaned as the ice shifted. A large boulder broke from the wall and rolled down past the balloon, shattering on the icy floor below. "Now, I must say good-bye and good luck."

As the balloon touched down deep inside the canyon, near the trunk of the giant tree, Celia turned to her brother.

"Still bored?" she asked.

He swallowed hard. He wasn't the least bit bored anymore.

"Right," said Celia, taking her brother's hand. "Let's go find Atlantis." She nudged him forward.

"Hey, why do I have to go first?" he asked. Celia raised her eyebrows at him. "Oh, right."

"Mm-hmm," she said and stepped onto the ground after him. They stood side by side and watched as Odd's balloon lifted off again, rising between the walls of ice and disappearing over the edge.

The twins stood still a moment longer. The air was warming at the bottom of the canyon, so they lowered their hoods and listened. The ice creaked and groaned. Oliver's head snapped from side to side with every noise, thinking he'd heard the roar of a dragon. Or a herd of dragons.

He wondered if dragons went in herds. Or was it flocks? Or packs, like wolves?

"Do you remember your catchphrase?" he asked Celia.

"It's not fair?" said Celia.

"No, the other one."

"Oh, yeah," said Celia, with a long exhale. "Let's get this over with."

30

WE SLEIGH A DRAGON

"THEY'RE TEARING THE place apart!" Dr. Navel watched on the little screen as Sir Edmund's thugs rampaged through the research station searching for Oliver and Celia. "I don't think they've even noticed the open kennel yet."

"Good," said Claire Navel. "We need to buy the twins as much time as possible."

"How far do you think they've gone?" said Dr. Navel. "It took Robert Peary's expedition over a month to reach the North Pole on dogsleds. And they were experienced and well supplied. Oliver and Celia have barely been gone a day. What we've asked of them is almost impossible."

"Almost impossible is a little bit possible." Claire smiled. "And where Oliver and Celia are concerned, I believe that *anything* is possible. They'll be just fine."

"How do you know?"

"I have faith, Ogden."

Dr. Navel furrowed his brow. He wasn't ready to surrender his children's lives to faith. He started absently flipping channels on the security monitor.

"Stop that," his wife said.

He didn't stop.

"Give it to me," she said.

He kept changing the channels. His wife reached over to grab the remote from him. He pulled it away. She reach for it again. He pulled it away again.

"Stop being childish," she said. She grabbed and caught it and they struggled over it for a few seconds, neither of them loosening their grip. Suddenly, the screen changed to a new image, an impossible image.

Oliver and Celia standing in an icy canyon, looking at a giant tree.

"Um." Dr. Navel dropped the remote.

"They made it!" their mother cheered.

"That's impossible," said Dr. Navel. "The distance . . . the tree . . ."

"*There are more things in heaven and earth . . . than are dreamt of in your philosophy,*" she quoted *Hamlet* at him again. "And we could sure help them out if we stole Sir Edmund's helicopter." She took a deep breath. "It's time."

"The Polar Plot?" he said, his eyes still fixed on the screen as Oliver and Celia studied the tree. He took a deep breath. The image vanished. They were staring at the hallway of the research station again.

Dr. Navel flipped the channel a few times, cycling through all the images, but he couldn't find the picture of Oliver and Celia again. He touched the screen and exhaled. "Let's do it." He braced himself. "I'm ready."

His wife smiled at him and touched his shoulder gently. "We'll get there," she said. "We'll help them."

Then she balled her hands into fists and punched her husband right in the stomach as hard as she could.

"Oof!" He doubled over.

"You okay?" She crouched next to him.

"One more time," he groaned. "It has to be believable . . ."

She punched her husband again. Sir Edmund was no fool. It had to look real. Dr. Navel was slumped on the floor, his face almost green. It was about as real as it could get.

"We're coming, kids," Claire Navel whispered, closing her eyes and thinking of her children. Then she rushed to the intercom. "Help! My husband! He's ill!"

"Quiet in there!" one of the thugs answered, his voice crackling with static.

"But he's really sick!" she said in her best whining voice.

"Who cares?" the thug answered. "Soon he'll be dragon food."

"What if he has a toxic parasite?" Claire asked. "You wouldn't want Sir Edmund's dragon to get sick. He'll probably take the cost of the veterinary bills out of your paycheck."

No answer came. Claire Navel waited, biting her lip.

"Just look on a security monitor," she said. "There's a camera in here. You'll see—he's really sick."

"Ugh," Dr. Navel groaned. He wasn't faking it either; his wife really could throw a punch.

The seconds ticked past like hours. They waited. Dr. Navel groaned on the floor; Claire Navel tried to look worried. It wasn't too hard. She was starting to get worried for real.

Then she heard the snap of a lock opening and chains falling to the floor. The door creaked open. As soon as the guard walked in, she karate-chopped him in the arm so he dropped his weapon, and then she elbowed him in the nose so he dropped to the floor.

"Nicely done." Dr. Navel pulled himself up, still clutching his stomach. A lump had formed where his head hit the floor.

"Good job writhing in pain." His wife kissed him on the forehead. "Now let's go."

They pressed themselves against the wall of the tunnel and scurried through the shadows. They ducked inside the rib cage of the pliosaur fossil when they heard Sir Edmund shouting from down the passage toward the cargo bay.

"Dogs!" he yelled. "You're telling me they set out on dogsleds! Who do they think they are? Dr. Frederick Cook?"

"Robert Peary beat Frederick Cook to the North Pole in 1909," whispered Dr. Navel. "That's who he means. Peary. Not Cook. Dr. Cook was a fraud."

"Now's not the time for that old argument," his wife whispered. "Come on."

"I'm on my way." Sir Edmund stormed through the passage, brushing right past the Navels hiding in the skeleton.

"We need to get to the lockers and put on some cold-weather gear," Claire Navel whispered. "Then we'll go to the helicopter pad."

"Can you fly a helicopter?" Dr. Navel asked.

"Of course, honey," she said. "Can't you?"

Dr. Navel blushed.

"It's okay." His wife patted him on the shoulder. "Maybe I can teach you someday, when the kids get their helicopter licenses."

"You think they'll want to do that?"

"I think they're starting to enjoy themselves with all this adventure. They just won't admit it yet."

"We'll see," said Dr. Navel. They crept to the lockers and dressed quickly in the first cold-weather gear they grabbed. Dr. Navel accidentally grabbed a ladies' parka, cut with luxurious curves, but they heard Sir Edmund's men coming so there was no time to change. They had to stuff themselves into a locker as one of the thugs came around the corner. He stopped right in front of their locker. They could just see his chest through the vents as he spoke.

"They've escaped!" he said. "The Navels have escaped!"

"I know that, you dolt," Sir Edmund snapped back. They could just see the top of his head through the vents in the locker. He was standing only inches away. "That's why we're looking for them!"

"Not the Navel kids, the Navel *adults*!" said the guard. "They knocked out Little Francis and escaped!"

"His name was Little Francis?" Dr. Navel whispered.

"Maybe that's why he was so mean," she whispered back.

"Idiots!" Sir Edmund yelled. "I am surrounded by idiots."

"Hey," said the guard. "I didn't do anything wrong. Don't yell at me."

Sir Edmund didn't answer. They could hear him breathing loudly. He was so close they could smell his terrible breath.

"Prepare the helicopter," he snapped at the guard. "The parents are of no concern to us right now. We have to stop the kids. I will not let the Navels beat me again. Once we have the children, the parents will fall in line."

They listened as Sir Edmund and his guard stomped off toward the helicopter pad. The tunnel fell silent again.

"What now?" said Dr. Navel. "They're taking the helicopter. The Polar Plot depended on that."

"We have to adapt, I guess," said Claire.

"I hate to say it, honey," said Dr. Navel. "But your plans and plots and gambits and ruses . . . they never seem to work."

"This isn't over yet," she said, climbing out of the locker. "Come on!"

The ran up the tunnel and out into the arctic air. Above them, they heard the rotor blades of the helicopter starting up. They rushed around the side to the staircase and took the steps two at a time, just as the helicopter lifted off. Sir Edmund saw them from the copilot seat and frowned. He shouted something into his headset.

"What'd he say?" yelled Claire Navel over the roar of the helicopter and the swirling snow.

"Duck!" shouted Dr. Navel.

"He told us to duck?" she yelled back.

"No," Dr. Navel yelled. "We have to duck! Duck!"

The back of the helicopter opened and one of

the henchmen leaned out with a rifle. Dr. Navel dove at his wife, knocking her off the helicopter pad and down into the snow below, just as the man opened fire. The bullets made a *twacking* sound as they plowed harmlessly into the snow. The helicopter banked hard to the right and lifted higher, flying away over the ice toward the North Pole.

Lying on the ground, the Navels watched the helicopter fly away and felt their hearts sink.

Just then, they heard the barking of dogs coming toward them. They looked up and saw a team of six sled dogs hauling a battered sled across the ice.

"That's Oliver and Celia's sled," said Dr. Navel in despair. "What's happened?"

The dogs rushed to where he was lying and started licking his face and barking. They jumped and spun in circles.

"Do you think—?" Dr. Navel wondered. "Do you think they'll take us to Oliver and Celia?"

"Yes," said Claire. "I think that's just what they want to do. Sled dogs are fiercely loyal. Come on!" She stood and raced back inside the research station.

"Wait! Where are you going?" Dr. Navel had to sprint after her.

"I just want to check one thing!" she called back over her shoulder. She ran right to the cargo bay, where the long crate with the dragon sat alone, unguarded and abandoned. It rattled slightly, held closed by the flimsiest of latches. "They just left the poor creature here. It would have been crushed when the station collapsed under the melting ice."

"What are you thinking now?" Dr. Navel asked.

"Dogs, a dragon, and the Doctors Navel," she said, hope creeping back into her voice. "I'm thinking I've got one more plan. What do you think of the Arctic Adventure?"

"If it gets us to Oliver and Celia," said Dr. Navel. "Then I love it."

Claire Navel cracked her knuckles. "I think we're gonna need a bigger sled."

31

WE'RE OVER THE RAINBOW

OLIVER AND CELIA had never seen a tree like the one at the bottom of the ice canyon before.

Of course, Oliver and Celia had never paid much attention to trees before, so it should not be terribly surprising, yet this tree was unique among all the trees of the world. In fact, some might say it was not a tree of the world at all, but a World Tree. In Norse myth, it held the worlds of gods, men, and monsters together.

Of course, it couldn't be *that* tree, thought Celia. That tree was just a story.

And yet, here they were, looking at a tree growing from a hole in the ice at the bottom of a canyon made of ice, floating on the ocean at the North Pole.

She supposed anything was possible.

Oliver went to the edge of the trunk, where it rose from the hole in the ice. The tree's bark was gold. It sparkled like it had been encrusted with diamonds, but it was smooth to the touch. The ice around the edge of the trunk played with the light, casting a rainbow down the center of the canyon above them.

"A rainbow bridge," said Celia.

"But it's not a bridge," said Oliver. "It's just a reflection from the ice."

"Maybe it'll lead to a bridge," said Celia.

"Maybe it'll lead to a dragon," Oliver grumbled.

"Only one way to find out where it goes." She started walking past the tree.

"I wouldn't go that way," a nasal voice said as she stepped forward. "That's the wrong way."

She looked around. She didn't see anyone but her brother. She took another step toward the trunk.

"He'll get you, but good!" the same nasal voice squealed.

"Stop that!" Celia scolded Oliver.

"What?" he said. "I'm not doing anything!"

"Did you hear that voice? That nasal voice?"

"What? No." Oliver listened just to make sure. "I don't hear anything. Just the creaking ice."

"Not now, a second ago. A voice. It warned me."

"No," said Oliver. "I didn't hear a voice." He shifted his weight from foot to foot. "Are you sure you're, um, okay? Did you get a toxic parasite?"

"I'm fine," said Celia. "Probably just nervous."

"That makes two of us," said Oliver. But I'm not hearing voices, he thought. He kept that thought to himself.

"Don't go *that* way!" Celia heard the voice again. She whipped around and saw a powder-white squirrel scurry up the trunk of the tree.

"There!" She spun Oliver around so he could see. "That squirrel! It just told me not to go this way!"

"The squirrel?" Oliver looked at his sister.

The squirrel stared back at the twins, sniffing the air with its little squirrel nose, but otherwise stayed completely still. It had two oversized front teeth sticking out of its mouth.

"Squirrels don't talk," said Oliver.

"You talked to a yak once," said Celia.

"That was in a dream."

"I talked to a giant squid when I was trapped on Sir Edmund's ship," said Celia.

"Yeah, but the squid didn't talk back," said

Oliver. "And anyway, that squirrel isn't talking."

Celia studied the squirrel. It wasn't talking. It was just a squirrel. It was strange that it looked the squirrel in the journal, and stranger still that it was on this mysterious tree growing from the ice on the North Pole, but it could not have talked. In spite of everything Oliver and Celia had seen, she knew that there were limits. Squirrels couldn't talk.

She turned her back to the tree and continued alongside her brother, farther into the canyon.

"He's gonna eat you!" Celia heard the voice calling.

"Okay! Enough! You stop that!" She whirled around and marched back up to the squirrel, who didn't move. "Squirrels don't talk!"

"Celia!" Oliver ran back to his sister. "You're yelling at a squirrel."

"I know I'm yelling at squirrel!" she snapped.

"Well, um . . ." Oliver scratched his head. "Is it, like, answering you?"

"Do you hear it answering me?" Celia said.

"No," said Oliver.

"Then I guess it's not, huh?"

"But I didn't hear it before either," said Oliver. "What'd it say?"

"It warned me that 'he' was going to eat me," said Celia.

"Who's he?"

"I don't know."

"Well, I guess you could, uh, ask?" Oliver suggested. He couldn't help glancing around again for hidden cameras. He had just told his sister to ask a squirrel for an explanation. This had to be an episode of *Bizarro Bandits*. Sometimes it felt like their whole lives were an episode of *Bizarro Bandits*.

Celia exhaled sharply. She didn't like the idea of asking a squirrel questions. Why would only she be able to hear the squirrel? Her brother was the one who believed in Santa Claus. If anyone should be hearing voices from talking animals, it should be him. She looked over at Oliver. He didn't hear anything. He was busy looking around the icy canyon for dragons . . . as if they were real.

"Oh, but they are real," said the nasal voice. "And the big brute's gonna swallow you whole!"

"Aha!" Celia turned back to the squirrel.

It scurried higher up the branch.

"Did it talk again?" Oliver wanted to know.

"You really couldn't hear it?"

"No," said Oliver. "What did it say?"

She thought for a second. If she told Oliver what the squirrel said, he'd probably freak out. He was freaked out enough already. Other than Beverly, he hated lizards. And a dragon was a giant lizard.

Maybe that was why only she could hear the squirrel. Maybe her brother couldn't handle it. She was three minutes and forty-two seconds older, after all. Perhaps that gave her certain talking-squirrel responsibilities. So be it. It was unfair, but she would shoulder her burden like any good sister should. She would protect her brother from the frightening news.

"Nothing, I guess," said Celia. "It must just be in my head. Squirrels don't talk. Let's go."

She turned her back to the tree once more and walked away.

"Nidhogg's his name," the nasal voice called. "Child of the trickster god! And he's as fierce as time itself! Little children are nothing to him. You'll be a snack before brunch!"

Celia ignored the voice and kept walking beneath the rainbow. She tried not to make a face like a squirrel was shouting at her in her head.

"Appetizers! Hors d'oeuvres! Tapas! Cheese puffs!" the voice called.

She set her eyes forward and walked faster.

"Why are you going so fast?" Oliver scrambled after her. "Slow down!"

He slipped and slid on the ice. He didn't like that his sister was acting crazy. She was supposed to be the one who kept *him* from acting crazy. If she lost her mind, they were both in trouble. He would have to do something to help her keep her wits. Arguing always helped.

"I wonder if this is where we'll meet Santa Claus?" he tried.

"Mm-hmm," Celia said like she wasn't even listening.

"I wonder if he's a bigger Corey Brandt fan than you?" Oliver continued, hoping to get some reaction from Celia.

"Mm-hmm," she said again. There was a loud crashing sound in the distance. Just ice falling, she told herself. It had to be just the ice.

"I'm glad Corey ended up with Lauren on *Sun-*

set High," Oliver declared, although he really didn't care.

"Whatever," said Celia.

"Okay, stop!" Oliver ran ahead and blocked her path. He stood right in front of her and put his hands out to the sides so she couldn't get past. "You don't believe in Santa Claus, you're the world's biggest Corey Brandt fan, and you'd fight a polar bear single handed if it said that about *Sunset High*. Why won't you argue with me? What's going on?"

There was another rumbling of shifting ice.

"We can't stop here," said Celia.

"You have to tell me what's going on first," said Oliver. "That squirrel really was talking to you, wasn't it?"

Celia nodded.

"And he said something scary, didn't he?"

Celia nodded again.

"And you didn't tell me because you wanted to protect me?"

She nodded a third time.

"Well, I don't need protection," he said. "I'm your twin brother, and if something bad is going to happen, I want to know about it."

"You sure?" said Celia.

"I'm sure," said Oliver.

"He said we were going the wrong way," said Celia.

"Is that it?"

"No." She sighed. "He also said there's a dragon named Nidhogg and he's going to eat us."

"And you believe him?" said Oliver.

"Why would he lie?"

"Why would he talk at all?" said Oliver. "He's a squirrel."

"So you aren't scared of a dragon?" Celia was surprised. "It's a big lizard."

"Sure I'd be scared if we saw one," said Oliver. "But I know the squirrel was lying."

"How do you know that? You couldn't even hear it."

"Because it said we were going the wrong way," Oliver said. "And we're not. Look."

He lowered his arm and pointed around the bend in the canyon wall. Celia peered around the corner and saw the rainbow go straight through an archway; on the other side, the canyon opened up into a huge chamber, ringed with a frozen moat. The rainbow disappeared right into a bridge of solid ice, and on the other side Celia saw the ruins of a frozen city.

Every building, every statue, every wall was covered in ice. Even the sky above was a dome of ice, although the light from the polar sun above made its way through, casting everything in a hazy blue. Small cracks in the ice above let light shine through, making more rainbows in the air above, like an underground light show.

"Very sci-fi," said Oliver.

At the start of the bridge was a large statue of a man with a trident, half crumbled, but it had to have once been Poseidon. There was a frozen moat ringing the outer wall and then a narrow strip of rough ground with icy buildings on it and icy statues of dolphins and sea monsters and men with squids for heads, and then another frozen moat with an icy bridge and another icy wall and on and on. The circles of walls and moats were nested, one inside the other, all the way to the center, where a great building lined with columns stood on top of an iceberg.

"Um," said Oliver, which Celia understood. He didn't mean "um." He meant, "I think we have just discovered the lost city of Atlantis frozen beneath the Arctic sea ice at the North Pole." He just couldn't find the words. "Um," he repeated.

"I guess people were right about it being underwater," said Celia. "If the ice all melted, it would be."

"Uh-huh," said Oliver, still at loss for words.

"Oliver, do you realize what this means?" Celia asked him.

"That we'll get our own TVs in our rooms?" he suggested.

"That the prophecy is true," Celia sighed. "We really are the greatest explorers in the world."

"Cool," said Oliver.

Celia glared at him. She didn't think it was cool at all.

32

WE'RE IN RUINS

AS THEY WALKED over the rainbow bridge into the city, frozen statues of men riding dolphins loomed over them. Crumbled buildings poked out of the ice, some with only one wall standing, others almost intact.

"I could really go for some cheese puffs right now," said Oliver.

"How can you think about food at a time like this?" Celia wondered.

"We just passed a bakery," said Oliver, pointing at one of the ruined buildings. It had no front wall, but along the side there was a big stone oven and three large flour mills. There was even a stone counter where customers must have once stood.

"It's creepy being in a ruined city that still looks like a city," said Celia.

"Look at that!" Oliver pointed to a small

building by the next moat. It looked like a gate-house, although the gate was gone. One wall was collapsed and inside they could see piles of spears lying scattered about, covered in frost. Oliver rushed over and tugged at one.

"Leave it," said Celia. "You don't know what kinds of crazy curses are on this stuff."

"You don't believe in curses." Oliver grunted and wiggled, trying to pull the spear free.

"Yeah," said Celia. "But you do."

Oliver grunted and let go of the spear. He couldn't get it loose anyway. He and his sister crossed the next bridge, inching along the slippery surface with their arms out at their sides for balance. Broken statues ran along the edge of the bridge, but was impossible to tell what they had once been; time, ice, and whatever calamity had destroyed Atlantis had erased the ancient sculptor's work.

On the other side of the bridge there were two tall obelisks rising into the air. They were covered in tiny hieroglyphics, obscured by a thick layer of ice and frost. Oliver tried to rub some off with his sleeve, but he couldn't get through it.

"Do you think our civilization would leave anything like this behind if explorers found us ten thousand years later?" Oliver wondered.

"No," said Celia, looking around at the new ring of the city they were on. "Everything we make is electronic. No one would even know what a TV was . . . it'd just look like some weird box."

"You don't think they'll have TV in the future?"

Celia shrugged.

"That's not a future I want to live in," said Oliver.

"Me neither," she agreed.

The buildings were bigger in this ring of the city. Some had columns holding up their front walls even though the rest of the building had collapsed behind them. Some had ornate fountains pouring solid ice and others still bore traces of brightly colored paint.

"So where do we find this library?" said Oliver. "I'm guessing they don't have a tourist information booth down here."

"It's probably that big building in the center of the city," said Celia. "If I were going to put a library down here, that's where I'd put it."

They made their way through the outer rings of the city toward the center. Celia felt more relaxed now. No dragons anywhere to be seen. She was silly to think there might have been. The squirrel had finally left her alone.

They reached the base of the tall hill where the big building sat. Big stone steps led up to the entrance, which was surrounded by columns. All along the steps were more obelisks, rising on every tier. A few had fallen over and broken on the ground, but at least a dozen were still standing.

"Here we go," said Celia.

"Yep," said Oliver, starting up the steps. She followed close behind, looking back as they got higher and higher to see the view over all of the ruined city. It was a series of circles, one inside the other, and as she'd thought, the buildings did get bigger and fancier the closer you got to the center. This hill must be the most important place. The perfect place to put the library.

She felt good about herself for figuring this out on her own. She'd done something no one else in the world had done . . . except that explorer whose journal she had. And her brother. But still, she felt special. Being the greatest at something felt pretty cool.

"Hey, I can see the hieroglyphics on this one," Oliver called from a few steps above her, rubbing off a thin layer of ice. Celia came up beside him. "I can't read them."

"We don't need to read any hieroglyphics," she said. "We just have to find the library." Celia went up the steps past him to the entrance to the building. "Come on!" she called again, rushing inside. Oliver stayed put to study the pictures on the pillar. He couldn't read the writing—it was all just lines and squiggles to him—but there were images that he could make out.

There was a picture of the great tree with a rainbow bridge running to the city ringed with moats.

Next to the tree, he saw the symbol of the Mnemones, the old-looking key, and he saw the symbol of Sir Edmund's Council, a scroll locked in chains. He was used to those symbols popping up everywhere. They were just like when you learned a new word, like enigmatic. You could go your whole life never hearing it, but then once you learn it, you start hearing the word all the time. Now that he knew these symbols, he saw them all over the place. And they were pretty enigmatic, he thought. Mysterious, but not really a mystery he wanted to solve.

He cleared more frost away from the side of

the obelisk and saw a picture of an island with a steaming volcano surrounded by giant squid. Again the symbols beside it. And there was another mountain with a picture of a monster, like the abominable snowman, the yeti that they'd found in Tibet, and another with a picture of a thick forest that, if he squinted, looked a bit like a jungle. And beside each picture, there were the symbols of the Council and the Mnemones.

He walked around the obelisk and cleared more ice away with his glove.

That's when his blood ran as cold as the frozen city around him.

He saw a picture of a man with a beard, just like the one in the explorer's journal, that he'd thought was Santa Claus. The man had two ravens on his shoulders and he flying through the sky in a basket. Oliver wiped away more ice. It was the basket of a balloon. The man's hair hung down over one of his eyes, just like Odd's.

Oliver felt his chest tighten and his heartbeat quicken.

Just below the picture of Odd were two small figures on the ground, each holding a spear, a boy and girl with dark hair and puffy clothes. They looked a lot like Oliver and Celia.

"Oh man," Oliver groaned.

In the picture they were fighting a dragon.

"Celia!" he yelled. "Celia, come here! Quick!"

She didn't answer him. She'd gone inside to find to the library and she couldn't hear him. In fact, at that moment, she was dealing with a terrifying discovery of her own.

The grand building at the center of Atlantis was empty. There was no library. Not even so much as a single book.

And the white squirrel was right beside her, his laughter echoing in her head.

"Told you so," he cackled.

33

WE'RE SQUIRRELED AWAY

"I TOLD YOU, you were going the wrong way," the squirrel's nasal voice rattled in Celia's head.

"You be quiet," Celia snapped. "You're a squirrel. You don't know anything."

"I know more than you do!" The squirrel laughed.

"You do not."

"I do too."

"You do not!"

"I do too!"

"Stop it!" Celia said. "Just be quiet."

"I'm not making any noise," said the squirrel. "I'm in your head."

"Well, if you're in my head, then you can't know more than I do." Celia crossed her arms, feeling triumphant until she looked over the empty room of icy marble again.

It was one big space with an altar at the far

end, where a statue had toppled over. The walls of the giant hall were also marble, although in places it had broken off to reveal crumbled stone beneath. There were a few other fallen statues in the room, broken monuments to gods and heroes that history had long ago forgotten. There were no passages or hallways or nooks where a library could be hiding. There were no shelves or books. There wasn't even a symbol of the Mnemones or the Council.

Celia couldn't believe that they'd come all this way for nothing. How would they ever save their parents now?

"Pardon me for being so rude." The squirrel scurried around the base of a statue that might have once looked like dolphin. Or a swan. It was hard to tell with ruins. Celia wasn't an expert on these things. She didn't care to figure it out. "My name is Ratatosk, and I am very pleased to meet you."

Celia huffed. She didn't answer. She was not about to be friendly with a figment of her imagination, especially after it had laughed at her and then acted like a know-it-all.

"I wouldn't go acting so high and mighty," said the squirrel. "If I'm only in your head, how did I know that you were going the wrong way? Hmm, smarty? Figure that one out!"

"Maybe because I sort of already knew there'd be no Lost Library," said Celia. "Because I never really believed in all this stuff anyway and you were, like, my own mind telling me what I already knew."

"You watch *The Daytime Doctor*, don't you?" he asked.

Celia nodded and then realized she was nodding at a squirrel and stopped herself. Of course, the squirrel would know that she watched *The Daytime Doctor* because he was her hallucination. He knew everything she knew. She'd just gone crazy like one of the losing contestants on *Bizarro Bandits*.

"Another explanation is that you aren't crazy at all," the squirrel said, hearing everything she'd been thinking. "Perhaps I really am talking to you in your head. And if I was telling the truth when I said you were going the wrong way, then . . ." The squirrel raised its voice to a high pitch, trying to get Celia to finish his sentence.

"Then what?" she said. "Stop being so enigmatic!"

"Guess."

"This isn't a game show. I am not guessing."

"Just try!"

"No!"

"You're no fun," said the squirrel, and just like that he scurried away, up the pillar, along the frozen ceiling, and out into the ruins of Atlantis.

"Hey, tell me!" Celia shouted after him, but his laughter was the only reply she received. She was left standing alone in the great empty temple, wondering what the talking squirrel could have meant. "If he was telling the truth about us going the wrong way, then . . . what?"

"Celia!" Oliver called, running inside. "Celia, we've got to get out of here!"

"There's no library," she told Oliver. "Look."

"I see that!" he said. "The squirrel wasn't lying!"

"I know," said Celia. "We were going the wrong way."

"Not just that!" Oliver cried. "About the dragon! They're real! And if we don't get out of here, we're going to have to fight one!"

"Oh come on!" said Celia, who was really quite sick of all this nonsense. "Are you hearing voices too now? We can't both be crazy!"

"No, it's, like, a prophecy! First, Odd flew us

here, then you talked to a squirrel, and now we fight a dragon! I saw it on an obelisk outside!"

"You can't believe everything you see on obelisks," said Celia.

"Come on," said Oliver, dragging her outside to see the hieroglyphs. When they got to the top of the stairs, overlooking all of Atlantis, Celia stopped. "Just down here," Oliver pulled her forward, but she resisted.

"I believe you," she said, pulling back against him.

"Just like that, you believe me?" Oliver stepped closer to her. Maybe she had gone crazy. She'd never believed him about anything so easily before.

Celia nodded and raised her finger, pointing across the city. Her face had gone the color of ice. Oliver looked over the ruined buildings of Atlantis, its frozen moats and crumbling bridges, and he saw what had frightened Celia. His shoulders slumped.

"Oh great," said Oliver. He really hated lizards.

And a dragon was a very big lizard.

34

WE THINK DRAGONS
ARE A DRAG

THE GREAT LIZARD came scrambling across the ruins of Atlantis, its yellow eyes fixed upon the temple steps where Oliver and Celia stood. It had a body like a snake, long and thick, but it also had four muscular legs and its massive claws crushed entire buildings like they were made of tissue paper. From where the twins stood, the city looked like a miniature model being attacked in a cheesy sci-fi movie.

The dragon flapped its leathery wings as though they were encrusted with ice and it couldn't fly. A cold wind swirled in the great cavern and knocked boulders of snow from the high walls above.

The dragon roared, the air filled with its piercing cry, and the twins pulled each other to the ground, expecting a jet of hot flame to come

bursting their way. When they were not bar-
bequed, they looked at each other and shrugged.

"I guess dragons don't shoot fire in real life,"
said Oliver.

"There shouldn't be any dragons in real life,"
said Celia.

"I liked it better as bones frozen in a wall."
Oliver was sure this had to be a relative of the
pliosaur whose fossil they had seen in the research station.

"The squirrel told me that this one's name is
Nidhogg," Celia told him.

"It has a name? Why does a giant lizard need a
name?"

"You've got a name, why shouldn't it?"

"Don't defend the lizard," said Oliver. "It's going to eat us."

"No," said Celia. "We're going to get out of
here. Come on."

She pulled her brother to his feet and they ran
down the steps, hoping to lose the dragon in the
narrow streets of the ruined city. The dragon
roared and changed course to follow them. Huge
chunks of ice fell from the ceiling, and the earth
shook as they ran.

"You've done it now!" the squirrel said, running along the rooftops by their side. "He slept for thousands of years, you know? I bet he's very grumpy to be woken up by little morsels like you!"

"Shut up!" yelled Celia.

"I didn't say anything!" yelled Oliver.

"Not you." Celia pointed up. "The squirrel!"

"He's talking again?" said Oliver. Celia grunted in the affirmative. "Ask him where we can hide!"

"Too late!" Celia called.

The dragon leaped into the middle of the boulevard behind the twins, half running, half slithering straight for them. They turned a corner and dove behind a marble column that had fallen across the street. They pressed themselves against it and held their breaths. The dragon clomped past, the foul stench of eons rising from its scaly feet as it stomped by the other side of the pillar.

Its footsteps faded.

Oliver exhaled.

The dragon's head snapped up over the building. With a roar, it leaped to the street in front of them.

"Aaaaa!!" The twins jumped up and ran,

sprinting back out onto the boulevard, racing toward the icy bridge to the next ring of the city.

"Ha-ha!" the squirrel laughed. "You'll never get away!"

"Help us!" Celia shouted.

"Me?" the squirrel scoffed. "But I'm just a dumb squirrel, remember? How could I possibly help you? You know *everything*."

"Okay!" Celia yelled. "I admit it! You aren't in my imagination. You're real and you know more than I do and I need your help!"

"Oh, that's priceless," laughed the squirrel. "The know-it-all admits she doesn't know it all! You're as good as gold, Celia Navel. Just as good as gold!"

Cackling, the squirrel scurried up the side of a building and raced away from them.

"Wait!" Celia called after him. "Help us!"

"I just did," the squirrel called back before disappearing into the city.

The twins kept running. The dragon crashed around corners and plowed through buildings. They ran over bridges and through old houses, but no matter where they tried to hide, the dragon found them.

Their legs burned and their lungs ached. They

dove behind the base of a statue that looked a lot like the mailman, Odd.

"That looks like—" Celia began.

"Yeah, I know," said Oliver. "I don't think Odd was totally honest about who he really was."

"We gotta remember never to accept rides from strangers in balloons," said Celia. "That should be a new rule."

"Yeah, I think—" Oliver stopped. The dragon snaked down the street behind them. It sniffed at the darkened doorways of old buildings, then slithered down a side street, growling and hissing.

"This really makes me miss Beverly." Oliver sighed.

"This makes me miss Mom and Dad," said Celia. Oliver looked at her, raising an eyebrow.

"I know," she said. "They get us into trouble all the time, but they usually have an emergency parachute or something. It's like, adventure isn't so bad when they're around."

"Yeah," said Oliver. "I kind of like adventure when they're around, actually."

"Okay, well that's crazy talk," said Celia.

"You're calling me crazy?" said Oliver. "You talked to a squirrel."

"Yeah." Celia grunted. "And some help he was."

"What'd he say?"

"He just made fun of me and called me a know-it-all."

"We gotta go back to that tree where he told you we were going the wrong way," said Oliver. "Maybe we can find the right way to go. Maybe we can still find the library and save Mom and Dad."

"What about the dragon?" Celia wondered.

"I've got a plan," said Oliver.

"Your plans don't usually go well for us," said Celia.

"This one will," said Oliver. "I'm calling it the Atlantis Antic."

"You sound just like Mom."

"Thanks." Oliver smiled and took his sister's hand. She nodded. They ran for the bridge over the moat at the outermost ring of Atlantis.

A screech pierced the air. The long scaly body of the dragon roared overhead, flying.

"I guess its wings thawed!" said Oliver.

The dragon landed in front of them on the opposite side of the bridge, blocking their way back to the tree.

"Now would be a good time for your plan," said Celia.

Oliver pulled his last bag of cheese puffs from his pocket.

"That's your plan?"

"Everyone likes cheese puffs," said Oliver, tearing open the bag. The dragon cocked its head to the side.

"We're doomed," said Celia. "Your plans really are just like Mom's."

Oliver pulled out a bright-orange cheese puff and held it aloft. The dragon's eyes narrowed to slits. Oliver tossed it and the dragon's tongue shot out and snatched the cheese puff from the air. It vanished into the great beast's maw without so much as a crunch.

"See?" said Oliver. "Now that he's got a taste, he'll want the whole bag."

Oliver wound up his arm and threw the bag as hard as he could off the side of the bridge so it slid along the icy surface of the moat away from them. The dragon watched it slide, made to move after it, but then took another deep sniff of the air and let the bag go.

"But . . . but," said Oliver. "No one can resist eating the whole bag!"

The dragon roared.

"I think this dragon can."

"But everyone loves the golden crunch of cheese puffs!"

"Oliver," said Celia. "That's it!" She reached into her pocket.

"What's it?"

"The golden crunch! That's what the squirrel said to me!"

The dragon stepped toward them, placing a wary foot on the icy bridge. The twins stepped backward. The dragon moved closer. Its mouth opened to reveal hundreds of needle-sharp teeth covered in hot drool and a tiny trace of cheese puff dust.

"I thought the squirrel called you a know-it-all!"

"It did," said Celia. "But it also said I'm good as gold."

"Yeah," said Oliver. "Dragons love gold. Mom said that when she was being all mushy about Dad!"

"Looks like one of Mom's plans worked after all." Celia pulled their mother's golden ring out of her pocket. It shined in her palm.

The dragon eyes widened. So did Oliver's. The

giant lizard and the boy stared at the ring, mouths agape. Celia bent back her arm and tossed the ring over the bridge. It arced through the air faster than the lizard's tongue could catch it and slid across the ice even farther than the cheese puff bag.

The dragon screeched and flapped its mighty wings, diving after the gold. It landed with a crash onto the surface of the moat, smashing its claws over the ring. It tilted its head back and roared in triumph.

Then the air echoed with a loud crack. The surface of the moat crunched. Little lines spread out beneath the dragon like a spiderweb.

The moat shattered and the dragon plunged down into the frozen water below. It flapped its wings too late. Ice coated them almost instantly and the weight of the ice on its wings pulled the great beast down. The dragon vanished in the blackness.

"Guess the dragon didn't know the rule," said Oliver. "The ice always breaks."

"We did it!" Celia jumped for joy. "It's gone."

Oliver, resting his hands on his knees, looked back at his sister and let out a long groan. "Why'd you have to go and say that?"

"What?" Celia shrugged. She pointed at the dark hole in the ice. "He fell in. We won."

"Celia!" Oliver shook his head. "You never say 'we won' after the monster falls into darkness . . . that's rule number one!"

"Oh . . . right," said Celia.

"Yep," said Oliver. He took a step backward. "He'll be back right about . . ." Oliver took another step backward. "Now!"

Sure enough, the dragon's head broke from the ice with a earth-shaking cry. Its head and claws slashed about through the air. Ice and snow flew in all directions. The twins dove flat against the bridge as the dragon thrashed in anguish. Its eyes met theirs and grew wide, a terrible hunger aimed toward them.

The dragon's tongue shot out in their direction. Celia dove over her brother, covering him with her whole body and covering her head with her hands.

There was a splash and then silence.

"Are we alive?" Oliver muttered from beneath his sister.

She waited, listened. Nothing.

"I think so," she whispered.

"Then can you get off me, please?"

"Sure." Celia rolled off her brother and slumped back on the bridge. They looked over the broken moat together. The water was still, the jagged edges of ice glistened. The dragon was gone. And so was the bag of cheese puffs.

"Told you so," said Oliver.

"Don't be a know-it-all," said Celia, helping her brother stand and holding his hand as they stumbled out of Atlantis back toward the World Tree.

Celia knew what they had to do now to save their parents.

"If there is a Lost Library hidden down here," said Oliver. "Then you have to ask that talking squirrel where to find it so we can save Mom and Dad."

It didn't sound any less crazy when her brother said it out loud.

35

WE CHECK OUT A BOOK

THE SOUNDS OF groaning ice, shifting and stirring, echoed around them as they crept along the canyon. Powdery snow fell from the upper walls and sparkled down through the rainbows above and covered them with a fine, wet dust. They followed the rainbows all the way back to the great glimmering tree. Oliver stopped dead in his tracks. Celia bumped into him from behind.

"Oof," she grunted.

"Not oof," said Oliver. "Odd."

"Good to see you again," said the enigmatic one-eyed mailman. Odd was crouched on the ground, feeding cheese puffs to the buck-toothed white squirrel. He stood and brushed the long hair back from his face, studying the twins through his good eye. "You two look a mess," he said. "I guess you met old Nidhogg."

"You knew there'd be a dragon!" Celia shouted.

"Like, a real, giant, lizard-faced, needle-toothed, gold-loving dragon!" Oliver added.

"And you left us here alone anyway!" Celia marched right up to look him directly in the face, although, given his height, she was actually looking directly into his chest.

Odd shrugged. "There's a prophecy. I knew you'd be fine. And someone needed to take care of that dragon. I never could."

"You aren't a mailman, are you?" said Celia.

Odd shrugged.

"Are you . . ." Celia looked around and dropped her voice to a whisper, even though there was no one but her brother and a sarcastic squirrel to hear her. "Odin, the All-Father?"

"I have many names," said Odd.

"Maybe he's Santa Claus!" said Oliver.

"He didn't say he was Santa Claus," said Celia.

"He didn't say he wasn't!" said Oliver.

"He said he has many names," said Celia. "They could be, like, Charlie or Milo or Snotface McGee. Why'd you jump right to Santa Claus?"

"You brought it up," said Oliver.

"I brought up Odin, the Norse god of war," said Celia.

"Well, I think he could be Santa Claus too."

"There's no such thing!"

"Uh-huh."

"Nuh-uh."

"Uh-huh."

"Nuh-uh."

"Uh-huh!"

"Why would Santa Claus want us to battle dragons?" said Celia. "He's a Norse god."

"He's Santa Claus."

"If he were Santa Claus, he'd have presents." Celia crossed her arms in triumph.

Oliver wrinkled his brow. His sister had a point.

"Oh, but I do have presents." Odd laughed. The twins turned back to look at him. Oliver smiled. Celia scowled. "Doubt is a good thing, children," Odd added. "Doubt leads to questions. And questions are the first step on any journey."

The twins rolled their eyes in unison.

"Enigmatic much?" Oliver scoffed.

"If you could be more obvious, we'd really appreciate it," Celia told Odd. "A dragon just chased us through Atlantis, so we're not in the best mood. We need to find the Lost Library to save our parents. If you can't help us do that, it doesn't really matter if you're the Norse god Odin, Father Christmas, or the tooth fairy."

"Well, there is no such thing as the tooth fairy," Oliver muttered under his breath. Celia elbowed him in the side.

"Oh, I like your brother," the squirrel chuckled.

"Quiet or I'll turn you into a scarf!" Celia snapped at it and the squirrel bolted up the tree, peering nervously around the trunk.

Odd cocked his head at Celia, puzzled.

"She's just yelling at the squirrel in her head," Oliver explained.

"Ah yes." Odd nodded. "He likes to pick on ones who think they're clever. He's a pest, but an amusing one."

"See!" said Celia. "I'm not crazy. He does talk."

"So you think you're clever?" said Oliver.

"I am clever," said Celia. She was glad to have it confirmed, even if it was by a mystical talking squirrel living under the ice at the North Pole.

"You just think you are," said Oliver. "If you were that clever, we'd have found the Lost Library by now."

"But you have," said Odd. "That's my present

to you. I needed someone to defeat that pesky dragon. Now that you have, I'd be happy to show you the place you seek. It's right below you." He pointed to the hole in the ice where the tree trunk grew. "Just climb down."

"Down?" said Oliver. "Isn't it just, like, the ocean down there?"

"Oh no," said Odd. "You really do have to see for yourself."

Oliver and Celia looked at each other and looked back at the tree. Celia nodded and Oliver stepped forward. He was nervous, but he didn't mind going first. He was about to see the place his mother had dreamed of for all this time. He just wished she were here to see it with him.

He wrapped himself around the trunk of the tree, like he was hugging it, and started to shimmy down the narrow space between its golden bark and the hard ice.

"Are you coming with us?" Celia asked the mysterious bearded man.

"I would never miss a chance to go to the library." Odd smiled.

Celia hugged the tree and shimmied down after her brother. She didn't have to go far before the hole opened up and she was sliding down the trunk into another great room of ice. Its walls were round, but there were no shelves. There was only a pedestal in the center of the room, and on it, a single big book, covered in a fine dust of snow. The curved ice reflected the book over and over and in all directions, so it looked like there were endless rooms with endless copies of the book sitting on pedestals in the center.

"This isn't a library," said Oliver. "It's just one book."

He went over to it and saw that there was a heavy golden seal on the cover in the shape of the Mnemones' key. He was about to open the massive book when Celia grabbed him.

"Careful!" she said. "Isn't it one of your rules that this will be booby-trapped?"

Oliver nodded. In movies, the mysterious thing on a pedestal was always booby-trapped. He guessed if he lifted it up poison darts would shoot out or the floor would collapse or there'd be some kind of curse.

"Well," said Odd, dropping into the room. "What do you think?"

"We think it's booby-trapped," said Celia.

"It's not booby-trapped," said Odd. "You've seen too many movies." He strolled over to the book and flipped it open. "Take a look. This is the Codex."

"What's a codex?" said Oliver.

"It means book," said Celia. *"A codex and a book are the same if you look."*

Odd raised his eyebrow. *"Wally Worm's Word World?"*

Celia nodded.

"Why not just say book then?" Oliver grunted.

Odd didn't answer him, just urged them to step up to the giant tome, which was yet another word for book, but no one really uses it, except when they don't want to say the word *book* over and over again.

The twins stepped forward and saw that the writing on the pages was just squiggles and lines in all directions, a jumble in black and gold and silver.

"What language is that?" Oliver wondered.

"Do you know the Sumerian myth of Enmerkar and the Lord of Aratta?" Odd asked them.

The twins stared back blankly.

"The tales of the Scythian king Fénius Farsaid?"

Again, the twins stared blankly at him.

"The Tower of Babel?"

"I know that one," said Celia. "The story that ancient people all spoke one language and they built a tower up to heaven, but the tower was destroyed and they were punished by having their languages broken apart so they couldn't understand each other."

"That's right," said Odd. "Many cultures have these stories of an original language, spoken by all in a time before time."

"He's talking like a fortune cookie again," whispered Oliver.

"Your brother's not the sharpest sword in the Viking horde, is he?" The squirrel was back, scurrying around at Celia's feet, laughing. "I've seen walruses with a quicker wit than he's got."

Celia tried to step on its tail. "Don't talk about my brother that way!"

"Did he just insult me?" Oliver wondered.

"Uh-huh," said Celia. "But it's not true. You've got more wit than a walrus."

"I sure do!" said Oliver, tired of being called dumb. He tried to step on the squirrel's tail too. Odd watched them chase the little creature around the room a moment before he clapped his hands once. It echoed like thunder. The squirrel froze and looked back at Odd, wide eyed.

"Enough," said Odd. "If you do not choose to keep quiet, I will silence you myself."

"Me?" said Oliver.

"Me?" said Celia.

"The squirrel," said Odd.

The little squirrel ducked its head and scampered off again.

"You two mustn't take it so personally," Odd told them. "In all our lives there comes a time when the gossip of squirrels will trouble us, and we must do our best to ignore it."

"I don't think most people have to listen to the gossip of squirrels," said Celia.

"I dunno," said Oliver. "Sixth grade's kind of like that."

"True," Celia said.

"Where were we?" wondered Odd.

"Tower of Babel," said Celia.

"Ah yes," said Odd. "The Ur language. The mythic language from which all others spring."

"Yeah, sure," said Celia.

"This is that language," said Odd, pointing at the squiggles and lines in the book. "This codex contains the root of all books. It can be read front to back, back to front, side to side, or on a diagonal. It can be read upside down or every other word, or in any pattern you can imagine. Or in no pattern at all. Because its possibilities are endless, so are the books it contains."

"Huh?" said Oliver.

"It's an infinite book," said Odd. "It is a book that contains all books, depending on how you read it. Every truth and its opposite are in this book. It literally contains all books that have been written, will be written, or could ever be written."

"Huh?" Oliver repeated.

"The myths of ancient Babylon, the tales of Homer, every romance novel," said Odd. "They're all in here, depending on how you read it. There's total gibberish and great literature."

"Or even a guide to raising Atlantis?" suggested Oliver.

"Exactly that," said Odd. "Instructions to melt the ice around us and bring the great city back to rule over a flooded world. That's in here. So is a guide to stamp collecting. Anything you can think of is in this book. This is what your old explorer found and hid in this place. You see, your mother's theories were wrong. The Library of Alexandria really was lost. It was destroyed just as history tells us it was, but everything that was in it is in this book, created long before the time of Alexander, long before history was even recorded. This book is the infinite memory of humanity, every story, every dream, every idea that is possible, and every idea that is impossible. The answer to any question at all is right here in front of you."

"So it's like our universal remote control?" said Oliver. "Works anywhere and can access anything, if you know what all the buttons do."

Odd wrinkled his one visible eyebrow. He had no idea what Oliver was talking about.

"Does anyone know how to read this book?" asked Celia.

Odd shook his head. "Not a living soul."

"Just like our remote," muttered Oliver.

"Hold on a second!" Celia stomped her foot. "We've been searching the world all this time, getting thrown out of airplanes and fighting monsters and grave robbers and evil billionaires just to find a book that no one knows how to read?"

Odd nodded.

"That is so unfair!" she groaned.

"No," a voice behind her sneered. "*This* is so unfair."

The twins turned to see Sir Edmund with three of his henchman standing by the trunk of the tree, pointing guns in their direction. "You'll give me that book now, I think."

He nodded for one of his henchman to take it from Odd. The henchman grunted under the book's weight. He lugged it back over to Sir Edmund and held it while the little man flipped through the pages, studying the symbols.

"You have no idea what you're doing," said Odd.

"Oh, I think I do," said Sir Edmund. "I'm taking the most priceless artifact in the world from two silly children and a strange old mailman who has gone very far off his route."

"He's no mailman," said Oliver, defiant.

"Shh," Celia hushed her brother. She didn't want to lose the element of surprise. Surely the mystical old man had a trick up his sleeve. He was the *deus* in their *deus ex machina* after all.

"Well, whoever he is," said Sir Edmund, "I hope you'll enjoy each other's company. Because I've rigged the canyon walls with dynamite. It should detonate in . . ." He pulled his phone out of his pocket and pressed a button. "Fifteen minutes. You'll be sealed in here for eternity. Sorry, kids. You won't be seeing the season finale of *Celebrity Fashion Crimes*."

"I don't like that show anyway!" Oliver shouted as Sir Edmund's henchmen hooked him to a harness and hoisted him back up the tree trunk. Then they attached the heavy book to a rope and started heaving it up, moving as fast as they could.

Soon Odd, Oliver, and Celia were alone in the empty room.

"Why didn't you stop him?" Celia whirled around on Odd. "I thought you were a mystical god or shaman or something!"

"I don't need to stop him," said Odd.

"Yeah," said Celia. "I think you do."

"Did you notice the cover of the book?" said Odd.

"Yeah, it had the Mnemones' symbol on it," said Oliver. "So?"

"It's gold," said Odd.

"So what does that—" Oliver stopped. He looked back at the tree and listened. "Oh," he said. In the distance, they could hear the sound of breaking ice. "I guess Nidhogg's finished his cheese puffs."

36

WE'RE GOOD AS GOLD

THE BOOK WEIGHED much more than Sir Edmund had imagined. It was about as tall as he was and also about as thick. His men struggled to heave it up the tree, back into the upper canyon. He tapped his foot and twirled his mustache while he waited for them. Ropes hung down the canyon walls from above, where he could just see the rotors of his helicopter waiting for him. It was only a matter of a few minutes before victory was his.

Once he had the book, of course, he'd have to find someone who could read it, but he had super-computers and hundreds of highly paid experts at the ready to crack that book and give him, well, everything!

"Aren't you proud of yourself?" A voice behind him snickered.

He spun around. "Who said that?" His head

darted from side to side. "Who? Show yourself!"

"Who! Who!" The voice laughed. "I'm no owl!"

He looked up and saw a white squirrel with buck teeth perched on a branch of the tree above him. He glared at it while it chewed a nut. Sir Edmund squinted at it a moment, then shook his head. Squirrels don't talk, he thought.

"Are you going to ask how I got a nut all the way up here on the North Pole?"

Sir Edmund spun around again, looking for the joker who was playing tricks on him.

"Navels? Are you there?"

"It's me, you dolt!" the squirrel shouted. "I'm right in front of you!"

"Squirrels do not talk!" Sir Edmund shouted at it.

"And yet here you are talking to me."

"I am not talking to you anymore."

"Your loss," said the squirrel.

"Nonsense," said Sir Edmund.

"It's not a nut, you know," said the squirrel, nibbling. Sir Edmund couldn't see its mouth moving. It was like the squirrel was speaking to him in his head. The squirrel just nibbled away at a little orange nut. "It's a cheese puff."

"Rubbish," said Sir Edmund.

"Oh, it's quite tasty," the squirrel said.

"Quiet!"

"Okay, but I was going to warn you about the danger you're in."

"Poppycock!" yelled Sir Edmund.

"Here there be dragons!" The squirrel laughed.

"I captured the last dragon years ago, just a runt, a baby, not a hundred miles from here," Sir Edmund declared. "It was the last of its kind, alone on the ice. There are no more dragons in the north."

"But who do you think gave me the cheese puff?" The squirrel swallowed the last bit, its buck teeth stained orange.

"Dragons do not eat cheese puffs!"

"Everyone eats cheese puffs!" said the squirrel.

"Uh, sir, you okay?" His men were next to him, panting from the climb up the tree with the heavy book. They looked concerned.

"You got a toxic parasite or something?" one of them asked. "You're yelling at a tree about cheese puffs."

"I am not yelling at a tree." Sir Edmund straightened his coat. "I am yelling at a squirrel." He pointed up to an empty branch.

His men glanced nervously at each other.

"There was a squirrel!" Sir Edmund said. "Oh, whatever! We haven't got time for this. Come on. We have to get out of here before the dynamite blows."

He turned to the wall of ice and started to buckle himself into another harness so his men could hoist him up, when the canyon echoed with a terrible roar. His men pressed close to each other.

"Relax," said Sir Edmund. "It's just the ice shifting."

Next came a shriek.

"That must be the shriek of a gentle snowfall," mocked the squirrel.

"Shut it, squirrel!"

Sir Edmund's men were frightened, as any sensible henchman would be, finding himself stuck in a canyon of ice at the North Pole with a devious billionaire who had gone as mad as a contestant on *Bizarro Bandits*.

We should note that, among henchmen, *Bizarro Bandits* is just as popular a show as it is among tweens.

There was a sound of shattering ice, boulders fell from above, smashing into the trunk of the tree, and a shadow passed over the canyon. Sir Edmund and his men looked up and saw the colorful underbelly of a giant flying lizard hanging above them.

His henchmen dropped the book and ran, darting beneath the rainbows toward the ruins of Atlantis.

"Cowards!" Sir Edmund yelled, unbuckling himself as quickly as he could and racing to grab the book from the ground.

The dragon reared back its head and howled, then dove toward him. Sir Edmund jumped, arms wide, mustache flapping, and pounced flat on top of the ancient codex. "I can't carry this tome myself!"

See? Tome is just another word for book.

The dragon just missed him, pulling up at the last moment and flying straight above him after the three henchmen. It scooped them up into its gullet as easily as Oliver tossing a handful of cheese puffs into his mouth. Henchmen, however, do not have a particularly satisfying crunch.

The dragon looped up again into the air, rising head over tail and twisting around again, landing face to face with Sir Edmund. Its giant head dwarfed the billionaire's entire body. His mustache twitched. The dragon snorted once and, it must be said, its breath was even worse than Sir Edmund's.

Sir Edmund started to inch backward on top of the book, dragging it with him toward the wall of the canyon. "Good lizard," he said. "Nice lizard."

The dragon matched him step for step. Sir Edmund heaved the large book in front of himself like a shield and peered out from behind its glittering golden cover. He fancied himself an expert in cryptozoology—the study of mythical beasts—but had no doubt forgotten the most basic fact about dragons and their love of gold. Had he done his own research (or ever bothered to watch an episode of *Beast Busters*) he would have known that hiding from a dragon behind a sheet of gold was like hiding from a teacher behind a blank quiz paper. That is to say, pointless.

"Now you back off!" Sir Edmund yelled. "I have one of your dragon kin as my prisoner and if you try anything, I'll—"

The dragon roared and knocked Sir Edmund backward off his feet. The book fell down on top of him, pinning him beneath it. His arms and legs splayed out to the side and his head popped

out from the top. He struggled and grunted, but could not free himself from beneath the weight. He tried to pull his phone from his pocket to call for help, but it was smashed.

The dragon moved above him, pouring rivers of hot dragon drool over the golden cover and soaking Sir Edmund's head. His mustache sagged.

"Oh! The gold! Of course!" Sir Edmund remembered too late. "You want gold! I have lots of gold! Tons of it! Let me go and I will come back with more gold than your lizard brain has ever dreamed!"

Of course, as Oliver could have told Sir Edmund, you cannot reason with a giant lizard. Lizards were like sisters. They want what they want and usually got their way. And right now, this ancient lizard wanted to eat.

Sir Edmund turned his head away from the dragon's face and saw Oliver, Celia, and Odd climbing up the tree trunk.

If there had ever been a time when he was truly glad to see the Navel twins, it was at that moment.

"Help!" he cried. "Help!"

He saw Oliver and Celia look at each other and sigh.

They started having a conversation. What could they be talking about at a time like this? Did that mean they were going to save him? Or that they wanted to watch him get eaten?

He really wished the Navel twins wouldn't be so enigmatic.

37

WE TIE THE KNOT

OLIVER AND CELIA shimmied up the golden tree trunk as fast as they could, but when they reached the top, they froze. The dragon had broken from the ice and towered over Sir Edmund and his stolen book just a few feet from them.

"It's—" Oliver started but Celia shushed him.

The dragon hadn't noticed them yet, and she'd prefer it if her brother's big mouth didn't announce their arrival.

"We can't just stand here," whispered Oliver. "The dynamite could blow anytime."

"We need to get past somehow," Celia whispered back.

Sir Edmund's head turned and his eyes met theirs. "Help!" he cried. "Help!"

Oliver and Celia looked at each other and sighed.

"The dragon's going to eat him," said Oliver.

"He was going to leave us for dead," said Celia. "And he's tried to kill us before."

"Plus all the stuff he did to Mom and Dad," added Oliver.

"Yeah," said Celia. "But isn't there some rule about this?"

"Yeah." Oliver sighed. "If we want to be the good guys, we have to help him."

"Do we want to be the good guys?"

Oliver and Celia looked back at Sir Edmund, with foreheads wrinkled and lips pursed.

He smiled meekly in their direction.

They rolled their eyes.

"I guess," said Oliver.

He and his sister sprang into action.

"Hey, dragon!" Oliver shouted, running around the tree. "Over here!"

The dragon roared, still rather cross about being tricked into the moat, and charged toward them. Odd dove out of the way as the great lizard charged and the twins ran around the tree. The dragon snapped at them, just missing as they took cover on the opposite side of the trunk. It darted around the tree and they ran ahead of it, spinning the monster in circles.

"I've got a plan!" Oliver yelled as they ran.

"Not again!" Celia yelled back.

"This is a good one!" said Oliver. "It's called the Norwegian Knot!"

"Why does it need a name?" Celia stumbled, but Oliver caught her hand and pulled her up so they could keep running the dragon in circles.

"I named it with a silent-letter word!" said Oliver. "Plans with silent letters have to work!"

"That's not a rule!"

"It is now!" said Oliver. "Keep running the dragon in circles!"

They raced around the tree trunk again and again and again. They got dizzier and dizzier, but so did the dragon. It began to smash into the walls of the canyon, losing its footing and flapping its wings, but still it circled, chasing Oliver and Celia. Someone watching from above might not have been able to tell if the dragon was chasing the Navel twins or if the Navel twins were chasing the dragon. In fact, the circle chase had grown so close that the twins were nearly stepping on the dragon's tail.

"When I say jump, jump!" Oliver yelled.

"You just said jump!" Celia yelled back.

"Not that time! The next time I say jump!"

"Now?"

"No, not that time either!"

"Stop being enigmatic!"

"Now!"

Oliver jumped forward, catching onto the dragon's tail, and Celia jumped forward, catching onto Oliver.

"Oh!" he yelled. "Don't pull me off!"

In a rage, the dragon lunged at them, and Oliver shoved himself off the other side of the tail, pulling his sister with him. They hit the snow with a thud and rolled away. The dragon's head roared and shot out toward them. Just as its jaws were about to clamp down, devouring the twins in one gooey bite, it came up short. Its head snapped back. It writhed and wiggled just a few feet from where they lay. It snapped at them but couldn't reach.

Oliver smiled.

"It worked." Celia gasped. "I can't believe it worked."

The dragon had tied itself in a knot around the great golden tree. When Oliver and Celia dove off its tail, it dove right under itself. With every lunge, the knot only grew tighter.

"See?" Oliver panted. "I'm nothing like Mom. My plans work."

"Not quite." Celia pointed. Sir Edmund had slithered out from beneath the giant book and was trying to tie a rope around it to haul it out of the canyon.

"Odd," Celia yelled. "The book!"

"Celia," Oliver yelled. "The dynamite!"

An explosion tore the ice near the top of the canyon. A dozen boulders, each the size of big-screen television, crashed down, blocking the path that led back toward the ruins of Atlantis. Another explosion next to the first sent a torrent of ice and snow raining down on the tree.

"You have to go!" Odd rushed over to the twins and picked one of them up under each of his arms. He dragged them to the ropes. "Climb!" he yelled. "Climb!"

"Why is survival so much like gym class?" Celia wondered.

"What about you?" Oliver asked.

"I think I'll stay down here a while. That lizard and I have some unfinished business."

"But you'll be trapped forever!"

"I highly doubt that," said Odd. "Someone will always be along in time."

"Oliver, come on!" Celia started up, hand over hand.

"He's being all enigmatic again!" said Oliver, following his sister.

The explosions had set off a cascade in the old ice. The outer walls of the canyon were collapsing in toward each other. The crack in the ice was closing up like a zipper, filling in the entire canyon. Sir Edmund was struggling on his own rope, barely a foot off the ground, unable to lift the weight of the universal book.

"Leave it!" Oliver called. "You'll be trapped if you don't leave it!"

"I've come too far to give up now!" Sir Edmund yelled. "I will get this book! I will control everything! I will not be beaten by two lousy coach potatoes!"

"We're not couch potatoes!" Oliver yelled.

"We're audiovisual enthusiasts!" Celia yelled.

"And the greatest explorers in the world."

Celia looked at her brother; he smiled as he climbed. She figured she didn't have anything else to add.

They climbed as quickly as they could; below them they heard the roar of the dragon and the grunts of Sir Edmund.

"Hurry!" Celia yelled. The avalanche was rushing at them, filling in the crack. They saw

Sir Edmund's helicopter tip forward and ride the rushing snow down into the abyss in a shriek of twisting metal. Sir Edmund didn't even look up at it. He was hauling himself slowly, hand over hand, red faced with the strain of the book dangling from a rope on his waist.

The twins still had a few feet to go to reach the top. Oliver climbed with his hands and legs, inching up. Celia pulled ahead of him. She reached the top first, threw her arms down, and grabbed her brother. She pulled and lifted him the rest of the way. His foot snaked out just as the crack smashed shut in a burst of snow.

They slumped backward together on the ice. Above them was a striped barber's pole covered in frost. It had a sign on it that read:

THE NORTH POLE ~~IS~~ *WAS* HERE.

"Why's it say *was*?" wondered Oliver.

"Because the ice is always drifting," said Celia. "The North Pole is just a spot on the ocean. The ice floats above it."

"I think Sir Edmund got smushed by the ice," said Oliver.

"We did our best to save him," said Celia. "He wouldn't have done the same for us."

"I guess he gets to spend forever with that book he wanted so badly."

"Yeah," said Celia.

"I guess Atlantis drifts with the ice," said Oliver.

"I guess," said Celia.

"So was it just luck that we found it?"

"What do you think?"

Oliver didn't have an answer. Destiny. Accident. There wasn't much difference when it was done. The twins lay in silence a moment, listening to the crackles and groans as the ice floes at the North Pole shifted and settled again.

"Sir Edmund should have watched more movies," Oliver said after long consideration.

"What do you mean?" Celia sat up.

"His last words were pretty lame," Oliver said. "The last thing he ever said was 'couch potatoes.'"

Celia nodded. "You know, if we hadn't made it out, your last words would have been 'greatest explorers in the world.'"

Oliver shrugged. "We found Atlantis," he said. "And that universal book."

"But no one else will ever see them. They're

sealed up under all this ice. And it's always moving."

"Yeah, but *we* saw them," said Oliver. "And that's pretty cool."

"I guess so," said Celia.

"Mom'll be disappointed."

"If we ever see her again." Celia looked around. Other than the barber's pole that had been set there by some previous explorer, she saw nothing but rough ice in all directions. There were boulders and ridges where other floes had smashed together, and little channels of water where the ice had pulled apart. There were no other canyons, from what she could see. Maybe that crack opened just for us, she thought. Destiny.

"So what now?" said Oliver. "I don't think we can walk all the way back to the research station."

Celia stood and helped her brother up. "We won't have to." She smiled and pointed toward the horizon. A strange creature was racing at them, half running and half flying over the frozen landscape. It looked like a little version of the dragon they had just trapped in the ice, but it had lots of little strands hanging off of it and it was pulling an odd bundle with many heads. It was moving so fast that the bundle didn't even hit the ground. It sounded like it was barking at them.

"Is that a *deus ex machina*?" asked Oliver.

"No," said Celia, squinting and shading her eyes with her mittened hands. "I think that's Mom and Dad."

38

WE'RE NOW HERE

THE SLED BOUNCED along the ground, smashing through piles of snow and rattling from side to side. As it drew closer, Oliver and Celia recognized it as their old dogsled, except the dogs were riding inside with their parents. It looked like their mother and father had tied the harness ropes to what could only be a baby dragon, dragging them in a mad flight to the North Pole.

Oliver turned to his sister. "How come I can go my whole life without seeing a single dragon, and then I see two in one day?"

"I guess that's what being an explorer is all about." She shrugged. "New experiences."

"Right . . ." Oliver nodded, considering it. "It's not too bad."

"If you like that sort of thing," finished Celia.

The baby dragon charged straight for them.

Their mother and father, both holding the reins, heaving back, pulled the dragon to slow it before it crashed into the twins. It had a large steel bit in its mouth that was actually a piece of the steel research station door.

The dragon skidded to a stop just in front of the twins. Its long body curled around itself, coiling like a snake, and it lowered its head to study them.

Their parents' sled careened sideways, spilling both parents and sled dogs across the ice like a scattered bag of cheese puffs.

The dragon sniffed at them. Its eyes narrowed to slits. It shrieked.

Oliver, still distrustful of lizards, jumped behind his sister. Celia, still unwilling to back down to an animal, no matter its size, didn't even flinch.

"Down there." She hitched her thumb toward the scar in the snow where the canyon had sealed itself up again. The dragon sniffed at the ice, gave a nod, and bolted up into the air, trailing the empty dogsled behind. It turned and shot straight down, boring into the ice like a drill and vanishing beneath the surface.

"How'd you know it wasn't going to eat us?"

Oliver asked, still squeezing onto Celia's shoulders.

"It was just a kid," said Celia. "All it wanted was to go home."

"Oliver! Celia!" Their father brushed himself off and raced over to hug them. "You're okay!"

Their mother ran to them, squeezing them from the other side so their faces were squished together in a hug, like two ice floes crashing into each other. "I knew you guys would be all right!"

"How'd you know that?" Oliver grunted.

"Duh!" said Celia. "Destiny."

"Well, sure," said their mother. "And this." She pulled their universal remote control from her pocket. "It turns out, watching TV comes in handy."

"Told you so," said Celia.

"Did you see that?" Their father laughed, hugging the twins when their mother was done. "We rode in on a dragon! Dragons are real!"

"We know," said the twins in unison.

"We named this one Brandon," said their father, still smiling.

"So?" Their mother looked all around them at the endless field of ice. She glanced at the old

North Pole sign. She turned back to her kids. "Did you . . . find anything?"

"Were we supposed to be looking for something?" Celia scowled.

Her mother's shoulders slumped.

"Kidding." Celia shook her head. "Jeez, Mom . . . so serious."

"We totally found Atlantis." Oliver smiled.

Their mother's expression brightened.

"It was a ruined city below the ice, with moats and statues and obelisks," Celia explained.

"And dragons," said Oliver.

"And talking squirrels," said Celia.

"There was a squirrel, anyway," said Oliver.

"It talked," said Celia.

"Just in your head."

"That's still talking."

"It kind of isn't."

"It is."

"It isn't."

"It is!"

"And the library?" Their mother stopped their argument. "Did you find the Lost Library of Alexandria?"

"Not exactly," said Oliver.

Their mother frowned again.

"But we found something even—" Oliver started, but Celia elbowed him in the side.

"We didn't find it," she said.

"But we—ow!" She elbowed Oliver again.

Oliver furrowed his eyebrows at her, but he couldn't tell what she was thinking.

"Hmm," said their mother.

"We don't have to worry about Sir Edmund anymore, though," Celia added. "He came after us, and well . . ." She nodded toward the mound of ice where the canyon used to be.

"I did the Norwegian Knot!" Oliver boasted. "It worked!"

"So, I guess you'll want to keep looking for the Lost Library?" said Celia. She watched her mother's face closely. A flicker of doubt ran across it, but then she shook her head.

"No," said Claire Navel. "Maybe some questions are better left without answers. Anyway, I think I've been gone long enough. It's about time we do like that dragon and go home."

Celia smiled. That was what she wanted to hear. Oliver grinned from ear to ear.

"By the way," their mom asked. "How did you guys get all the way here without your dogsled?"

"Odd brought us," said Oliver.

"Odd?" Their father looked around.

"He's a mailman," said Oliver.

"There are no mailmen at the North Pole," said Dr. Navel.

"Well, he wasn't really a mailman," Celia explained. "He was more like—"

"An enigma," smiled Oliver.

"Exactly," said Celia.

"The problem with an enigma," said their mother, "is that it won't help us get home. We need a ride."

"But we're in the middle of nowhere," said Celia.

Dr. Navel raised his finger in the air and smiled. "Remember that *nowhere* also spells *now here*!"

"Not now, honey." His wife patted him on the back. "If we stay out here too long, we'll freeze or starve . . . or both."

"That's not the worst of our problems," he told her.

"Freezing and starving sound like pretty bad problems," said Celia.

"I agree." Their father nodded. "But getting eaten is surely worse."

The twins and their mother followed Dr. Navel's gaze to the hungry polar bear loping toward them across the ice. It had traveled for days pursuing their scent and it was not about to give up now.

Oliver rummaged through his pockets, hoping for one last bag of cheese puffs to give the bear. His pockets were empty. The dogs started barking, but the bear kept coming.

"We could really use a fighting walrus about now," said Oliver.

"Walruses don't live this far north," said Dr. Navel.

"Of course not," said Oliver with a roll of his eyes. "Why would nature want to help us out?" He turned to Celia. "We could really use one of your *deus ex machinas* now."

"They're not my *deus ex machinas*," said Celia. "They're just a thing that happens. And on TV, they only happen once. I think we already used ours up."

"Mom? Dad?" Oliver looked to his parents.

"Don't worry," said Dr. Navel. "We have never let you get eaten before. We won't let you get eaten now."

Celia had her doubts, and she was about to express them when the bear scratched at the ice and roared. Then, with the full of force of his thousand pounds, he charged the Navel family. Sometimes a polar bear likes to get the last word in an argument.

39

WE DON'T RUN AWAY

OLIVER AND CELIA'S parents threw themselves in front of the twins as the bear surged at them. Their father puffed out his chest and shouted. Their mother yelled and waved her arms.

"I think they've gone crazy," said Oliver.

"They're trying to establish dominance," said Celia. "To scare the bear off."

"I don't think it's working," said Oliver.

When the bear had closed the distance between them to a few feet, all six sled dogs jumped onto its back, snarling and biting into the tough fur. The bear thrashed and groaned, shaking and swatting the dogs off into the snow. The Navels turned, grabbed Oliver and Celia by the hands, and started running.

"We won't get away!" said Oliver.

"We've done this before!" said Celia.

"What about the dogs?" said Oliver, glancing back over his shoulder.

The bear hadn't given up on a meal of Navels. It was already in pursuit, even as the loyal dogs bit at its heels. They were slowing it down, never relenting, even as the bear's massive paws swatted them away as easily as we would swat at gnats. Of course, the Siberian husky, at sixty pounds of muscle and fur with powerful canine jaws, could be quite a bit more pesky than a gnat.

Seeing the Navels getting farther and farther away, the bear bellowed in frustration.

"We can't just let it eat the dogs!" said Oliver.

"It doesn't want to eat the dogs," his mother said, pulling him through the snow. "It wants to eat us!"

"No." Celia turned. "It wants to eat cheese puffs!"

"What?" Oliver spun out of his mother's grasp and watched the bear tearing at a giant pallet of cheese puff bags. The fur of its face was covered in orange dust. Plastic wrapping flew in all directions as it tore the bags apart. The dogs watched from a slight distance, ready to pounce again. The bear glanced back at them, suddenly indifferent, and dug back into its cheesy meal.

"I told you so!" said Oliver. "Everyone likes cheese puffs!"

"Where did that come from?" Dr. Navel marveled.

"There!" Celia pointed at the sky. A plane was circling around, dropping pallets of food from the sky. A whole case of beef jerky smashed into the ice, not far from the cheese puffs. The bear sniffed the air and trudged over to it, ripping into the dried-meat product with abandon. The dogs watched, licking their lips.

The plane had two large skis on the bottom instead of landing gear, and as it circled, it tipped its wings. They saw the initials C.B. painted on the side.

"That's Corey Brandt's private jet!" said Oliver.

"I guess we get a *celebrity ex machina*," said Celia.

"Is that a thing?" said Oliver.

"It is now," said Celia.

"I hope he lands in time." Oliver looked back to the bear, who had glanced up from its meal and turned toward the dogs. It stepped toward them slowly, its head lowered like it was stalking them.

"Maybe it didn't like junk food," said Celia, her heart thumping in her chest. The lead dog had its snout just inches from the bear's face. The bear lifted one of its paws in the air, preparing to swipe, and the dog stretched its paws on the snow in front of it, lowered its head, and lifted its back in a playful bow.

"Don't play!" Oliver shouted. "Run!"

The bear cocked its head. The dog wagged its tail. And suddenly, the bear rolled over on its belly, the dog jumped on it, and the animals did what comes naturally to anyone who has a full belly and nothing better to do: they played.

Within seconds, the other dogs had joined in, rolling and jumping around the bear in the snow, barking and yipping and swiping at each other without the slightest hint of violence.

"I guess they don't hold a grudge, huh?" said Oliver.

"The animal kingdom can teach us humans how to live," said Dr. Navel. "If only we could learn to heed their lessons and treat them with the respect and—"

"Da-ad," the kids groaned. "Can we please not have a explorer lecture right now?"

"Fine." He sighed, because if anyone had

earned the right to not learn anything else, it was Oliver and Celia. They had discovered Atlantis, after all.

The plane landed and the door opened. Corey Brandt, wearing custom-tailored cold-weather gear, stood smiling at the top of the stairs. "You like the duds?" he asked, showing off his outfit. "Corey Brandt's Polar Pants! Limited Edition!"

"Bwak!" Dennis the chicken clucked at his feet, wearing a matching sweater. Patrick the monkey screeched with glee, climbing onto the celebrity's head.

"Where's—" Oliver started, when he heard a loud hiss, and Beverly, the only lizard in the world that Oliver could stand, came scurrying toward him down the steps. It was like a scene from one of Celia's soap operas. Oliver ran toward her. She ran toward him. And then she stopped, frozen in place.

"Like all lizards, the *Heloderma horridum* is cold-blooded," said Dr. Navel. "She's in suspended animation now." Dr. Navel lifted Beverly by the tail. She was stiff as a popsicle. "She'll be fine once she warms up."

"I guess that's how the dragons live under the ice," said Oliver.

"Remind me never to warm up a dragon again," said Celia.

"So." Corey showed them all onto the plane. "Where to now?"

"We could go look for Sir Edmund's mysterious zoo," suggested Dr. Navel.

"I could show you around Hollywood," suggested Corey.

"I have a crazy idea," said their mother.

"Oh no," said Oliver.

"Oh no," said Celia.

"Let's go home and see if there's anything good on TV." She smiled.

Oliver and Celia exhaled. There was *always* something good on TV.

40

WE DON'T MISS A THING

"**TONIGHT WE PRESENT** this year's Explorers Club Award for Excellence in Exploration to the youngest winners in our club's history," Professor Rasmali-Greenberg declared to the packed Great Hall of the Explorers Club in New York City a few weeks later.

All the gathered adventurers, explorers, daredevils, and globe-trekkers burst into applause. Even the stuffed animal heads all over the walls seemed to smile down on the ceremony. In fact, the only explorers who were not smiling were Oliver and Celia Navel, standing on the stage at the front of the room.

"I can't believe we're the guests of honor at a Ceremony of Discovery," Oliver whispered to his sister.

"I can't believe we have to stand here the whole time," Celia grumbled back.

Their father and mother, each dressed in their finest outfits, cheered the loudest of all the explorers. Neither of them had ever been more proud. The Ceremony of Discovery was a time-honored tradition of the Explorers Club, where fortunes were wagered, discoveries declared, and honors awarded. Some of the greatest explorers ever to have held a compass had stood on this very same stage to receive this very same award. Dr. Navel kept using the sleeve of his tuxedo to wipe away his tears. His wife had to hold him steady.

In the crowd, Sam, who had come all the way from South Sudan, leaned over to whisper to a boy in the red robes of a Buddhist monk, who had come all the way from Tibet, who leaned over to whisper to a boy from the one of the last tribes of sea-nomads on earth, who leaned over to whisper to a girl in a fuzzy wool hat.

The girl, Oliver and Celia's friend Qui, nodded at the boys, all Oliver and Celia's friends from past adventures. She held her hands up in the air where Oliver and Celia could see them from the stage. She wiggled her fingers.

"That's the sign," Celia whispered into Oliver's ear. "It's time! We have to go!"

"We've haven't gotten our medals yet!" Oliver whispered back.

"And now," the professor declared to the room, "the medals!" He pulled two shining gold medals from a heavy wooden box. They each hung on bright-blue ribbons and they shined under the gleaming lights of the stage. Oliver's eyes widened.

"We're going to miss the beginning of the show!" Celia said.

"I want to get my Explorers Club Award for Excellence in Exploration medal," he answered.

"That's a stupid name for an award," said Celia.

"It is not," said Oliver.

"It is too," said Celia.

"It is not," said Oliver.

"It is too," said Celia.

"It actually is," said the professor, smiling down at them then turning back to the crowded room, holding the medals high in the air. "Which is why we are renaming it after our newest patron, whose generous donation to the club has paid for this glorious celebration! Let's have a round of applause for Mr. Corey Brandt and the brand-new Corey Brandt Prize for Excellence in Exploration!"

Corey Brandt strolled onto the stage, dressed in a crisp black tuxedo, sporting a brand-new hairstyle, which had quickly become the most popular hairstyle in the world, and big smile across his face.

"You guys are the best," he told the cheering crowd. He reached down and gave high-fives to some of the people in the front row. Madame Xpertina, world-famous trans-Siberian motocross racer, fainted. Corey Brandt had that effect on some people. They were usually teenage girls, but he had been famous for long enough not to be surprised by the occasional fainting trans-Siberian motocross racer.

"I'm thrilled to be here tonight," he said. "To, like, honor my friends, the two bravest kids I've ever met, Oliver and Celia Navel! The greatest explorers in history!"

He gave them a sideways wink and Celia couldn't help but wink back. Oliver gave Corey a thumbs up.

"I'm also excited," Corey continued, "that tonight we'll see the premiere of my newest made-for-TV movie, *The Accidental Adventures of Celia and Oliver Navel!*"

Again the whole room burst into applause, although this time Oliver and Celia happily joined in.

"If he doesn't speed this up, we're going to miss it," Celia whispered as she clapped.

"I can tell by their faces that Oliver and Celia are, like, so ready for this to be O-V-E-R, over." Corey laughed. Celia blushed and hoped the teenage superstar hadn't heard her. He rushed across the stage and shook each of their hands with a formal bow. Then he hung each of their medals around their necks and stood between them, raising their arms into the air above their heads like boxers at the end of a prize fight.

"Woo-hoo!" their mother cheered.

"Hurrah!" their father yelled.

Beverly hissed her lizard hiss and Patrick screeched his monkey screech and Dennis the chicken bwaked his chicken "bwak" from his perch on top of the head of a great stuffed polar bear by the door.

However, near the back of the crowd one man wasn't clapping. He didn't even seem to be paying any attention at all to the ceremony around him. It was easy not to notice him among the gathering of eccentric characters with odd haircuts and elaborate outfits. He wore a conservative black tuxedo, and if he had a strange haircut, one wouldn't know it, because he had a baseball cap pulled low over his head. He didn't look up from his phone, where he tapped away sending text messages, a gold ring glistening on his finger, inscribed with the symbol of a scroll locked in chains.

"Hey, Corey," Oliver said through his clenched smile, his hand still held in the air above his head.

"Yeah?" Corey said, his face locked in roughly the same expression as the crowd continued clapping.

"Can we go watch your movie now?"

Corey laughed and let go of their hands. He nodded and, with the explorers still cheering, led the twins off the stage and toward the door, where their friends from all over the world had gathered.

"Where are you going?" their father called out and the room fell silent to listen. The man in the baseball cap perked up, finally paying attention.

"We're going upstairs," said Oliver.

"But we haven't told everyone the story about how we freed the animals from Sir Edmund's zoo!" Dr. Navel threw his hands in the air, dismayed to think that his children hadn't changed at all, in spite of all they had been through.

"We want to watch Corey's movie!" Celia objected.

"It's your movie, guys," said Corey. "It's about you."

"You lived through it all in real life!" Their father shook his head. "Why do you want to watch it on TV?"

"Because, Dad." Celia rolled her eyes. "Stuff is better on TV!"

Their father sighed.

"Well." Their mother stepped up next to him. "Can we watch it with you?"

Oliver looked at his sister.

She shrugged. "Sure."

Their mother squeezed Dr. Navel's hand. "Family movie night," she said.

"That won't be so bad." Their father smiled. "I'll make popcorn."

"With nothing gross on it," said Celia with a firm glare.

"Fried beetles aren't gross!" Dr. Navel objected.

"We have them every time!" Oliver whined.

"Can't we just have melted butter?" Celia pleaded.

"Melted yak butter?" Their father raised his eyebrows.

"Fine," said the twins.

Their father jumped with glee.

The man in the baseball cap rolled his eyes and sent another text message: "NAVELS STAYING HOME. AGAIN. NO CHANGE."

His shoulders slumped when he read the text he got back. "KEEP WATCHING. WE WANT TO KNOW IF THEY TRAVEL."

"★" he answered.

Oliver and Celia nearly knocked over Professor Eckhart of the Department of Obscure Spiritualities as they rushed from the Great Hall. The crowd of adventurers, explorers, daredevils, and globe-trekkers were left muttering to one another in surprise. They'd never seen anyone abandon their own award ceremony before.

"You know," Corey told them as they raced toward the Navels' apartment on the 4½th floor, "if you like the movie, I could always make another one." He grinned back at Dr. and Dr. Navel. "If you have more adventures I can make it about . . ."

Oliver and Celia stopped and looked at each other. Their friends had already gone ahead of them to turn on the TV. Their parents were on the steps just below Corey and the walls all around them were decorated with pictures of famous explorers from times gone by.

Oliver raised his eyebrows at Celia, a hint of a smile forming at the corner of his mouth. His medal, like hers, shined on his chest.

"We'll think about it," she said, and they continued up the stairs to their apartment, where they could hear the music starting for the made-for-TV movie of the week. Their breath quickened. They had to move fast. They knew that if they ran up the steps two at a time, dodged past the rack of ancient spears, and dove through the door to their apartment with a somersault over the couch to the front of the TV, they might not miss the beginning of their story.

We should be happy to note that they didn't miss a thing.

A FINAL NOTE FROM THE AUTHOR

IT IS TIME, for now, to leave Oliver and Celia Navel in peace with their friends, their parents, and their cable television. But there is much more for us to discover!

You see, the search for Atlantis is almost as old as recorded history, and most of the theories contained in the story you have read are based on our research into the subject. Plato really did describe Atlantis and argue that it was a real place. Count Olof Rudbeck really did believe that the lost city of Atlantis was the same as the city of the Norse gods, led by Odin, and that its ruins really were to be found in his northern nation of Sweden, while other explorers have imagined that the North Pole is really the final hiding place of the Garden of Eden. Humans love hidden places and imagined lands, and we continue the search for our myths in the real landscape of Earth.

From Shangri-La to El Dorado to Atlantis, we have always been intrigued by places just beyond what we know, and nearly as soon as we think we've found one, we go on to think of others. We long for the blank space on the map to fill with our own dreams, and yet the known world is incapable of bearing our mysteries. Every time we make a discovery, we want to push on to the next one. That is the drive for exploration. There are many things in this book that are based on truth (including the ancient sea dragons!) and many that are pure fantasy. I hope your unanswered questions will lead you to uncover the truth for yourselves.

Or you could always see if there's anything good on television . . .

ACKNOWLEDGMENTS

BOOKS, LIKE ARCTIC expeditions, are supported by countless people who never get medals hung around their necks. They should. In lieu of a medal, there are a few people to whom I would like to offer my thanks.

The adventures of Oliver and Celia Navel would have remained unknown to the world but for the editorial sleuthing of Jill Santopolo, who has been their champion (and mine) since the beginning and whose hard work has made these books far better than I could have made them on my own. Her aide-de-camp (which is just a fancy way of saying adviser), Kiffin Steurer, has provided wonderful insights, and Michael Green, publisher extraordinaire, brought the tale to Penguin with great faith and enthusiasm. In fact, the entire Penguin family embraced Oliver and Celia with open arms. Thanks go to Casey, Jessica, Scottie,

Shanta, Marie, Katie, Annie, Cristin, Stephanie, Julia, Christina, and the rest of the marketing, sales, and publicity teams. Illustrator Jonny Duddle and the Penguin Art Department brought the images of the Navels' world to life, while the copyediting staff improved my writing in ways I cannot begin to express (but I bet they could!).

Penguins may be flightless birds, but I am now convinced they soar.

As always, Robert Guinsler's super-secret-agent experience makes my writing life possible (with a valuable assist from international woman of mystery Kelly Farber and woman of international mystery Aviva). Natalie Robin has long served as my narrative navigator, and I'd have been as lost as Atlantis without her.

The series was improved by Sam Cove and his family, as well as my earliest readers—Chris and Charlie Noxon, my sister, Mandy, and my brother-in-law, Dennis—who provided their own visions and prophecies when I needed mystical guidance. Mandy and Celia are very close kin, while Dennis is more heroic and kind than any chicken I could dream up. Of course, Mr. Xanders, my fifth-grade teacher who made me read *Redwall*, deserves some credit too.

Lastly, such a tale would have been impossible to tell without the care and support of Tim, who makes both adventures and excessive TV watching better, as well as his aide-de-camp, Baxter, a very wise dog indeed.

Turn the page to sample the first
Accidental Adventure:

WE ARE NOT EATEN BY YAKS

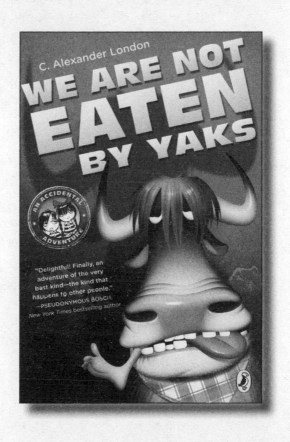

1

WE MEET THE
RELUCTANT RESIDENTS

IF YOU DID NOT KNOW what business took place inside Number Seven East Seventy-fourth Street, you might look up from the sidewalk toward the light flickering in an upper window. You might see two eleven-year-olds pass by that window, their faces pale and thin, with dark circles around their eyes, and you might imagine that they are the lonely and neglected children of wealthy socialites, forever trying to escape from their dull and pointless days.

But you'd be wrong.

Number Seven East Seventy-fourth Street is home to the old and exclusive Explorers Club, which is the most important society of adventurers, explorers, daredevils and globe-trekkers in the world. The two children who sometimes pass by the windows are reluctant residents of the 4½th floor of this club, and it is their story which concerns us here.

Now, most children would love to live on the 4½th floor of the Explorers Club. Most children would thrill to learn the mysteries and secrets shared among the explorers, and most children would love spending every evening hearing tales of danger and distant lands from the adventurers, explorers, daredevils and globe-trekkers who passed through those grand halls.

At least, that's what the adventurers, explorers, daredevils and globe-trekkers kept telling the Navel Twins.

Celia and Oliver Navel, it must be said, are *not* most children. They did not like mysteries or secrets, tales of danger and distant lands, nor did they like adventures or exploring, and certainly they *hated* trekking the globe. While other boys might have turned green with envy because Oliver Navel had celebrated his ninth birthday in a cursed graveyard on the edge of the Sahara Desert, Oliver turned green with a stomachache because of the sweet-and-sour caterpillar cake he was served, which tastes even grosser than it sounds.

And while most girls might have screamed with jealousy that Celia had been given a Mongolian pony for her sixth birthday, Celia could not stand the smell of horses. In fairness, I believe that the horse could not stand the smell of her either. Whatever the case, the horse had to be returned to Mongolia with a formal apology from the Explorers Club, and Celia Navel was banned from ever entering the country, which suited her just fine. She did not like wild animals or exotic places. Nor did her brother.

The Navel Twins liked television.

They liked television more than anything else in the world. They would watch for hours and hours without a break, and it didn't even matter what they were watching as long as the comforting glow of the TV flickered across their eyeballs.

That little box contained worlds! Nature shows gave them nature. Dramas gave them drama. And cartoons about talking llamas gave them talking llamas, which one could hardly find in the "real" world anyway. They never wanted to miss a show for anything as boring as school, or dinner parties or going outside to play, and definitely not for trips to places like Mongolia.

Unfortunately for them, Oliver and Celia lived at the Explorers Club with their parents, Dr. and Dr. Navel. Well, they actually only lived with their father, Dr. Navel, as their mother, Dr. Navel, had gone off to find the Lost Library of Alexandria, which she believed had never been lost, and had, herself, unfortunately been lost in the process. Though a search party searched for her, no trace had yet been found. Two of the explorers sent to find her even disappeared themselves.

Sometimes, when there was nothing to do during commercial breaks for one of their shows, the twins would talk about their mother.

"You ever miss her?" Oliver would ask his sister, popping cheese puffs into his mouth like it was no big deal, but really holding his breath for his sister's answer. Looking at Celia was almost like looking at a picture of his mother. Celia had the same little nose and giant eyes. She had the same pale skin and dark hair. Oliver had a face more like his father's, but his hair and eyes were the exact same as his sister's. Both of them had dark circles under their eyes from staring at the screen all the time.

"It's her own fault," said Celia. "If she'd just stayed home with us, she'd never have gotten lost."

"Yeah, but don't you think—"

"Shhh," Celia cut him off, "*Ten Ton Taco Challenge* is back on."

Oliver didn't say anything after that, because he loved *Ten Ton Taco Challenge* and because he could tell his sister didn't like talking about their mother. Oliver secretly missed his mother a lot. Celia's secret was that she hated *Ten Ton Taco Challenge*. She was only watching it now because the sound of frying tortillas kept her from thinking about the Saturday morning their mother left

"Good-bye, Oliver," she had said. "Good-bye, Celia." She kissed them each on the forehead.

"Uhuh," both kids grunted because cartoons were on and they did not appreciate interruptions. It was hours before they even noticed their mother had gone and taken her big backpack with her. She was always going off somewhere. That was the thing with having explorers for parents.

They were always coming and going, looking for the Ancient City of This or the Lost Library of That. Oliver and Celia could not have known that that kiss on the forehead was the last time they would see her.

Some kids might have taken a lesson from that, and stopped watching so much television, but not Oliver and Celia. After their mother left, they watched even more. A television could do a lot of what a mom did, anyway, like telling stories and keeping them company when they were lonely. And even better, if they got tired of it, they could just turn it off, which you couldn't do with a mom at all. Of course, they never did get tired of TV. It drove their father crazy.

"Too much television rots your brain!" he complained. He was standing in his usual spot behind the couch with his arms crossed in their usual upset way.

"No," Celia answered without looking away from the screen. "Mongolian Horse Fever rots your brain."

Dr. Navel sighed. Celia was right of course. She'd caught Mongolian Horse Fever from that horse he gave her for her sixth birthday. They'd barely gotten her to the hospital in time.

"Well," he said, changing the subject. "We have a dinner to go to. It's in honor of your mother."

The twins stood slowly. They couldn't argue with him about their mother. *Ten Ton Taco Challenge* would have to go on without them.

"Another banquet," Celia groaned.

"There will be a prince, and a hot-air balloonist, and a deep-sea diver," Dr. Navel said excitedly.

"Ugh," Oliver and Celia said together and deflated like two hot-air balloons crashing into the sea.

Read the second book

in the series:

WE DINE WITH CANNIBALS

Don't accidentally miss
this third adventure!

WE GIVE A SQUID A WEDGIE